VAMPIRE PARK

"How forgetful of me!" exclaimed Lord Freddie, slapping the palm of his hand against his forehead. "I haven't told you yet, have I, about my ingenious scheme?"

"No, Freddie," said the Count unsurely. "What ingenious scheme might that be?"

"This is really going to impress you, cousin," said Lord Freddie simpering proudly. "I'm going to turn Alucard Castle into a theme park."

"A *theme park*!" gasped Count Alucard.

BITE INTO THE VAMPIRE SERIES –
IT'S FANGTASTIC!

VAMPIRE PARK

Willis Hall

**ILLUSTRATED BY
TONY ROSS**

RED FOX

A Red Fox Book

Published by Random House Children's Books
20 Vauxhall Bridge Road, London SW1V 2SA

A division of Random House UK Ltd
London Melbourne Sydney Auckland
Johannesburg and agencies throughout the world

1 3 5 7 9 10 8 6 4 2

First published simultaneously in hardback and paperback by
The Bodley Head Children's Books and Red Fox 1997

Printed and bound in Great Britain by
Cox & Wyman Ltd, Reading, Berkshire

Papers used by Random House UK Limited
are natural, recyclable products made from wood grown in
sustainable forests. The manufacturing processes conform to
the environmental regulations of the country of origin.

RANDOM HOUSE UK Limited Reg. No. 954009

ISBN 0 09 965331 1

1

The rough-hewn wooden wheels groaned as they lumbered unwillingly along the uneven cart-track. The two bullocks strained at the harness as they struggled to pull the heavy cart across the bumpy forest floor.

"*Heave*, Ludwig! *Harder*, Osman!" cried the carter, flicking his long whip as he tried to coax his animals to greater effort.

"We should be able to see the lights of the village soon," said the passenger encouragingly.

The carter, whose name was Ernst Tigelwurst, did not reply. Instead, he glanced up nervously through the tree-tops at the darkening sky. The afternoon was drifting towards evening. The days were all too short at this time of year. Not for the first time, Tigelwurst wondered whether he had been wise in agreeing to take the man to the village of Tolokovin? He had been well paid for his trouble, true enough. Five grobeks were more than he would receive for delivering his entire load of lamp oil and chicken feed to the village store. What's more, the stranger had given him the money in advance – which was usually the sign of an honest man. All the same, it was not wise to take risks in Transylvania, particularly at the time of the full moon . . .

"It is certainly a delightful evening," professed the passenger, trying again to strike up a conversation.

"Very pleasant," said Ernst Tigelwurst.

The carter did not really want to talk to the stranger, but conversation provided him with the opportunity to turn and take a long hard look at his passenger for the very first time.

Ernst Tigelwurst had been hard at work humping heavy sacks onto his bullock-cart when the fellow had first approached him. Head down and busily employed, the carter had paid scant attention to the stranger's arrival on the scene. Then, when the man had held out the five grobeks in his open palm, Ernst Tigelwurst had been too overcome at his good fortune to consider what his benefactor looked like.

During the journey though, as the shadows had begun to lengthen, the carter had become increasingly nervous with regard to his passenger's identity. Now, as he allowed his eyes to stray over the man from head to foot, Tigelwurst began to suspect that he had made a very big mistake!

The man sitting at Ernst's side was wearing a black suit, a frilly starched white shirt and a white bow tie. He had a black cloak with a scarlet lining slung over his shoulders. An embossed gold medallion was suspended around his neck on a fine gold chain. But even more disturbing than the man's clothing was his appearance. He was tall, thin, pale-complexioned, with red-rimmed eyes and long jet-black hair which was combed straight back over his

head. He also had two pointy teeth that jutted over his lower lip – one on either side of his mouth.

There was one other all-important clue to the passenger's identity. When the man had told the carter that he had an item of luggage with him, Ernst Tigelwurst, pocketing the five grobeks, had helped him hump the big black box onto the back of the cart without so much as a second thought.

Now, as the sun dipped towards the rim of the distant mountain, Ernst Tigelwurst glanced fearfully over his shoulder at the sleek polished black coffin with its silver handles, tied loosely on top of the sacks of chicken feed with a length of rope.

What a fool he had been! Who else but a vampire would travel the world with a coffin? Vampires slept in their coffins, a man did not need to have studied at Frankfutel University to acquire that piece of knowledge.

Ernst Tigelwurst pondered upon all of these facts and then gave a little shiver. They were going to the village of Tolokovin which nestled at the foot of Tolokovin Mountain. Halfway up that mountain stood the dreaded Castle Alucard. "Alucard", as the carter knew full well, was "Dracula" spelled backwards. The stories about the Castle Alucard and the evil vampires that had dwelled for centuries within its ivy-covered walls were whispered fearfully all over Transylvania.

Children who did not obey their parents were told that, if they did not change their ways, they would be despatched to Castle Alucard for supper – not to *eat* that meal, but to be consumed themselves as part of it. Ernst Tigelwurst had suffered such threats himself when he had misbehaved as a child. He still woke up sometimes with a scream in his mouth at the prospect of such a punishment.

The carter decided that he needed to do something – and *fast* – to rid himself of his evil-hearted passenger, before the passenger took it into his head to do something nasty to Ernst Tigelwurst. Sheer desperation presented him with an idea.

"Mercy preserve us!" cried the carter, tugging hard on the reins and bringing the bullock-cart to a standstill. "Did you hear that?"

"No," said the passenger, raising his dark eyebrows enquiringly over his red-rimmed eyes. "What was it?"

"Why, it sounded like a cry for help," said Tigelwurst, pointing into the pine trees at one side of the cart-track. "And it seemed to come from over there."

"I can't *see* anything," said the black-garbed man, still puzzled and peering into the forest in the direction that Tigelwurst was indicating. "What sort of a cry was it?"

" 'Help me!' it sounded like," said the carter. "And then a pause and then 'Help!' again. I heard it quite distinctly. It was either a child's voice or a woman's. One of us ought to investigate. I'd go myself – except I think I should stay here and keep an eye on the bullocks."

"I'll go," said the passenger, slipping a lanky leg over the side of the cart and feeling for the ground with the pointed toe of one of his well-polished shoes.

A moment later, the black-cloaked figure was inside the rows of pine trees. Several strides of his long legs later, both the cart-track and the bullock-cart were lost from sight.

"Hello?" the man called out into the dark of the forest. "Is anyone there?"

But no answer came. The forest was silent – save for the "*Coo-coo-coo-ing*" of a wood-pigeon calling for its mate. And then more silence. And then the sound of some small woodland creature scuttling to its nest in the forest undergrowth. And then silence again.

"There's nobody here, my friend!" the passenger called out through the fringe of trees towards the cart-track. "Do you think that you might possibly have been mistaken?" There was no reply and the passenger called out again: "I say there! Carter? Can you hear me? Are you all right?"

"Cooo-COOO . . .!" went the wood-pigeon up in the tree-top, a little more angrily this time at not having had a reply.

"Gee up!" The carter's voice filtered faintly through the pine trees. The cry was followed by the distant sound of a cracking whip.

Sensing that all was not as it should be, the lanky figure turned and plunged awkwardly through the thick bracken and then stumbled out onto the cart-track.

Ernst Tigelwurst seated on his bullock-cart was lumbering off into the distance.

In the passenger's absence, the carter had quietly manoeuvred his bullock-cart in a U-turn on the cart-track. Then, after levering the coffin to the ground and tossing the rope down after it, he had shaken the reins and set off, as fast as the bullocks would allow, back along the path on which they had come. Tigelwurst had decided that the Tolokovin peasants would have to wait for another day for their delivery of lamp oil and chicken feed. The carter's only wish was to put as much distance as he could between his evil passenger and himself, and in as short a time as possible.

"*Heave*, Osman! *Pull*, Ludwig!" Tigelwurst's voice drifted back along the cart-track.

Count Alucard, the last of the vampires, for such was the identity of the despairing black-garbed figure, watched as the bullock-cart disappeared around a bend.

The Count made no attempt to call after the fleeing carter. What would have been the use? Had he so desired, the Transylvanian nobleman could have sprinted off on his long legs and caught up with the slow-moving bullock-cart in next to no time. But what good would that have done? The Count knew that he could not succeed in making the carter change his mind. When fear of vampires struck at a simple peasant's heart, there was little point in trying to argue sense or reason with him.

The sad truth of the matter was that Count Alucard presented no threat at all to any living creature. The Count was a life-long vegetarian. Although he had inherited his ancestors' abilities and could change himself into a nocturnal flying creature – when Count Alucard chose to use these mystical powers he became a harmless, furry, fruit-eating bat with an appetite for a juicy ripe nectarine or a plump fleshy peach. The very idea of him plunging his pointy teeth into a human person's neck was enough to make the Count squirm with disgust.

7

"At least the fellow's had the decency to leave me my coffin," sighed the Count as he glanced down at that item which the carter had dumped, unceremoniously, in the middle of the muddy cart-track.

Count Alucard shook his head and sighed again. Although the carter had done him a favour in dropping the coffin off his cart, he had also provided him with a problem. There were another three miles at least between himself and the village of Tolokovin – and then another mile's hard slog up the steep mountain road before he would be back home in Alucard Castle. It was hard to lift the coffin single-handedly off the ground, let alone carry it by himself.

Count Alucard was returning home after travelling aboard. Ernst Tigelwurst had been right in one thing he had said: the Count had been brought up to prefer his satin-lined coffin for a good night's sleep to the comforts of an ordinary bed. He had learned to do so as a child and it was too late now for him to change his habits. The coffin was doubly useful as it also acted as his suitcase whenever he went on his travels. He kept inside it all the necessities of life: clean clothes; night attire; a toilet-bag, and a six-pack of tomato juice which, when liberally doused with Worcester sauce and sprinkled with black pepper, was the Count's favourite night-time tipple.

But now he found himself abandoned miles from anywhere with the added burden of his coffin, the Count began to see himself as being in a hopeless situation.

And just when it seemed as if things could get no worse – as if to prove him wrong, it started to snow.

8

"Just my luck!" he murmured to himself as the soft white flakes swirled all around him and began to settle.

In ordinary circumstances, Count Alucard loved the Transylvanian snow. When he was home at Alucard Castle with a log-fire blazing in the Great Hall, there was nothing he liked better than to watch the snow showers drifting past the mullioned windows. But to suffer a snowfall *now* was a harsh blow indeed. Supposedly, the winter was over. He had come home in order to enjoy the first delights of spring – and now there was this late winter flurry just when he could best do without it.

"Life is extremely cruel," sniffed the Count, who was occasionally given to the odd burst of self-pity. "Here am I – without a friend to call upon – and now it appears as if even Dame Nature is conspiring against me . . ."

"Grrr-oooOOOWL . . .!"

Count Alucard started at this unexpected sound and then, quickly recovering himself, turned around to see two half-grown sturdy wolves peering out at him from the undergrowth on the fringe of the forest.

"Good evening, Ilya – to you too, Lubchik," said the Count, recognizing the pair immediately as belonging to the pack that hunted in the Tolokovin Forest.

The wolves wagged their tails and padded over to greet the Count. Ilya, the broader-chested of the pair, licked Count Alucard's hand while Lubchik, who was thicker round the haunches than his fellow wolf, rubbed a flank against the Count's trouser-leg.

9

Count Alucard knew each and every one of the
Tolokovin wolves. As a boy, feared and shunned by
the village children, the Count had sought instead
the companionship of wolves. He had grown up
with the wolf pack. They regarded him almost as
one of their own. He called them his "children of
the night" and, in his nocturnal bat-form, often
flitted overhead as the wolves raced in close formation through the dark of the forest.

"Well met!" As he spoke, the Count ruffled the
grey-white blaze of fur on each wolf's chest. "It
seems that I am not entirely without friends when
they are most needed."

"Ah-whooo-OOO . . .!" howled Ilya, throwing
back his head and baying at the setting sun, excited
by the encounter with the vampire count.

"Grrr-rrrRRR . . .!" growled Lubchik, equally

delighted and nuzzling his wet nose into the Count's clenched hand.

"But what brings you both to this part of the forest?" mused the Count. He neither needed nor expected any answer. He guessed that the two young wolves must somehow have chanced to stray from the pack and then lost their way. "Apart from good fortune for all three of us," he added as an idea suddenly occurred to him which would solve several problems at once . . .

"Glory to God!" gasped Eric Horowitz, the village shopkeeper, and his jaw dropped open slowly in amazement.

Horowitz had come out into the village street, the bell above his shop-door tinkling behind him, to see if there was any sign of Ernst Tigelwurst and the bullock-cart with his monthly delivery of lamp oil and chicken feed. Instead of which, a most curious sight had met his eyes.

Count Alucard led the way, his scarlet-lined black cloak billowing out around him as he strode across the layer of snow which was spread evenly across the village street. Behind the Count, their fur bedecked with frost and glistening like silver in the moonlight, came Ilya and Lubchik, tugging enthusiastically and like a pair of huskies at their makeshift harness fashioned out of rope. The harness was tied to the filigreed silver handles on either side of the coffin which was gliding easily over the snow. The Count's spirits sank as he glimpsed Horowitz through the still-swirling snow, standing outside the village store.

11

Count Alucard had hoped that he might succeed in passing through Tolokovin without encountering anyone. The villagers seldom ventured out at night. In bad weather particularly, they preferred to huddle round their pot-bellied stoves and entertain themselves with folk-songs – usually about death or even worse misfortunes.

The Count had taken the chance, because of the weather, of coming through Tolokovin rather than going the long way round and by-passing the village. But he knew full well that if he should chance to cross a peasant's path, he could expect the usual abuse they hurled at him.

"Vile satanic blood-sucker!" was one of their favourite taunts, or "Accursed evil one!" and, sometimes: "Murderous demon of the dark!" And, despite the fact that the Count was none of these things, they would sometimes go even further and dance up close to him dangling bunches of garlic in his face. Like all vampires, Count Alucard detested garlic.

If anyone should ask the peasants *why* they did these things, they would shrug their shoulders. They did them because they had always done them. Their ancestors had done the same to the Count's ancestors. So it was, so it had been, and so it always would be . . .

As the Count trudged through the falling snow, drawing closer to where the shopkeeper was standing, he steeled himself for the insults. Strangely though, they did not come.

"A very good evening to you, Count Alucard!" the shopkeeper called out politely. Then, having recovered from his original shock at seeing the wolves, he added: "That's a particularly fine pair of animals you have there, if you don't mind me saying so."

"N-n-n-not at all, Eric Horowitz," the Count stammered, hardly able to believe his own ears.

Then, as the Count, the wolves and the coffin moved past, the shopkeeper called out a friendly "Goodnight!" and went back inside his store.

Count Alucard did not have long to puzzle over Horowitz's odd behaviour. Further along the village street, another door was opening. The Count felt his heart sink into his shiny shoes as he saw Sergeant Alphonse Kropotel stroll out of the police station and stand under the flickering gas-lamp in the shelter of the verandah. Eric Horowitz might have acted out of character, he told himself, but there could be no chance that the police sergeant would do the same. Sergeant Kropotel was always eager to show how much he despised and loathed the Count. Kropotel would have jeers and jibes and insults to deliver a-plenty.

Again, Count Alucard prepared himself to receive the abuse.

"Greetings, Count Alucard!" called Sergeant Kropotel as he twisted one end of his waxed moustache between gloved finger and thumb, his medals gleaming in the gas-light. "I heard that you had been away – how delightful it is to welcome you back again! You must favour us with your delightful presence more often."

Lost for words, the Count nodded dumbly at the police sergeant as he stumbled past the station. Something very strange was going on. The Count had not the faintest idea why both the shopkeeper and the policeman were behaving in such a curious fashion. No doubt the reason would be made clear to him before very long. For the moment, though, he needed to reach Castle Alucard before the weather took a turn for the worse.

"Forward, Ilya! *Pull*, Lubchik!" cried the Count. Then, beckoning the wolves to greater efforts, Count Alucard struggled onwards, through the thickening snow, towards the end of the village where the road rose steeply as it zigzagged up the side of the mountain.

2

It's a long, long way from Tolokovin, in Transylvania, to the little town of Staplewood, in England, but the same moon shines down on both of those places.

And that self-same moon which lit Count Alucard's way as he plodded along the snow-covered cart-track with the two wolves and his coffin was also, and at that very same moment, casting a silvery glow over the white-bearded, red-cheeked plaster gnomes that populated the front garden at No. 42 Nicholas Nickleby Close, Staplewood.

Albert Hollins, who lived at that address with his wife, Emily, and their twelve-year old son, Henry, worked at Staplewood Garden Gnome Company Ltd – a factory which boasted it was the largest manufacturer of those ever-popular decorative items in the entire world. Because of his important post as assistant manager of the packing department, Mr Hollins was entitled to purchase the company's products at their wholesale price – which was why the front garden at No. 42 was not short on garden gnomes.

The Hollins family owned garden gnomes in all shapes and sizes. They had gnomes poised with garden-fork or spade clutched in their plaster

hands; gnomes peering expectantly around shrubs or plants and holding up painted lanterns; there were several gnomes who were seated on plaster mushrooms, dangling fishing lines over the Hollins' little garden pond.

"Turn left at the fish-and-chip-shop," Emily Hollins would advise anyone who was visiting them for the first time, "cross over to the right and then keep on walking down the Close until you come to a garden full of gnomes – and then you've found us."

Inside the Hollins' living-room, Albert, Emily and Henry were sitting down with the television switched off as they pored over holiday brochures. It was almost springtime – the season of the year when the Hollins' thoughts turned towards their summer holidays. It was the time of year when

Emily regularly raided the travel agents' shelves. Her foragings that day had resulted in the large pile of brochures which was stacked in front of them on top of the sleek, black-wood polished coffin.

Perhaps it would be wise, at this point, to pause from our story long enough to explain *why*, exactly, the Hollins family employed a coffin as a coffee table?

If any inquisitive neighbour or relative should chance to ask that question, Emily had an answer always ready on her tongue: "It goes so well with the piano," she would tell them, nodding at the dark-wood upright which had been bought for Henry to practise on.

But the real reason was a much more interesting one.

The coffin belonged to Count Alucard. Henry Hollins was the only boy in his class – probably in the entire world – who could boast of a Transylvanian vampire for a friend. Not that Henry showed off about that fact – on the contrary, he kept the secret inside the family.

The Hollinses had come across the Count on a camping holiday when they had lost their way in Europe and inadvertently put their tent up outside Alucard Castle. Henry Hollins and Count Alucard had taken to each other on sight and instantly become firm friends. They had met up again on several occasions since. The last time that the Count had visited England, circumstances had demanded that he make a hasty exit. In order that he might do just that, he had asked the Hollins family if they would be kind enough to take care of his coffin for him. Emily, who had been intending

17

to invest in a coffee table anyway, had immediately spotted the coffin's potential.

Since that day, Count Alucard's spare coffin had held pride of place in the Hollins' living-room. Emily dusted the coffin weekly, polished it once a month and polished, too, the silver coffin handles. Every fortnight, she washed and ironed the satin shroud contained within – in case the Count should turn up unexpectedly in need of a night's bed-and-vegetarian-breakfast.

At that moment, though, the coffin was proving extremely useful as a place to store travel brochures.

"Do you want to hear what I quite fancy?" asked Emily then, without waiting for an answer, she continued: "I quite fancy a couple of weeks in Morocco."

"What's Morocco got to offer?" asked Albert unenthusiastically.

"Sun, sea and sand – what more do you want?"

"We could get all those at Blackpool," said Albert, who happened to have a brochure for that holiday resort in his hand.

"Sea and sand, perhaps, but not sun – not *guaranteed*," replied Emily. "Besides, there are camels in Morocco. *And* belly-dancers. You like a belly-dancer, Albert. Remember that one we saw in Tunisia?"

Albert nodded and smiled wistfully at the memory of the Tunisian belly-dancer who had wobbled her ample stomach to the tune of "How Much Is That Doggie In The Window?" delivered on the mouth-organ by a small gentleman tourist from Stoke-on-Trent.

"So how about it then?" asked Emily. "Shall we settle on Morocco?"

"I'm not so sure we should make our minds up *quite* so quickly, Emily," said Albert, who was wondering whether camels combined with belly-dancers would offer him more entertainment than Blackpool's Pleasure Beach Big Dipper and Big Wheel? "What do you think, Henry?"

Henry Hollins shrugged. Personally, he would have preferred another trip to a certain region in Transylvania. But he knew that Tolokovin would need to offer more than a spooky castle and a wolf-inhabited forest, if it was to tempt his parents back again . . .

Released from the makeshift harness, Ilya and Lubchik stayed long enough at the castle gate to bid their goodbyes to Count Alucard before turning and loping off, through the snow and into the forest in search of the rest of the wolf-pack. The Count smiled fondly as he watched the pair disappear into the dark of the trees then, taking a tight hold on the rope, he set off into the castle courtyard, pulling his coffin behind him.

The snow had stopped falling some time before, leaving a smooth white carpet across the mountain. The night sky was cloudless and twinkling bright with stars.

Once inside the comforting safety of the castle's courtyard, Count Alucard came to a halt and let out a long sigh of relief. But the surge of joy he felt at being home was not to last. A twinge of fear shot through his body as he spotted an oil-lamp's orange glow through one of the ground floor windows. Not only that, but he could also make out the flickering shadows of firelight dancing on the ceiling. Even more puzzling still, he could hear the sad strains of a violin drifting out of the castle on the still night air.

There were intruders inside his ancient home!

But who would dare to enter Alucard Castle? The local peasants were far too fearful of the castle's vampire history to venture inside the ancient ivy-covered walls. And the peasants' fears were so well known throughout the land that no stranger ever dared to go within a mile of Castle Alucard.

Nevertheless, the Count knew that his eyes and ears were not deceiving him. There were intruders inside his ancient home.

The Count decided that there must be an entire gang of wrongdoers in the castle. For surely no one human being would wander inside a vampire's walls alone? And even though he sensed that there were several intruders, the Count still told himself that they were not lacking in bravery. For they had not only dared to enter the celebrated Castle Alucard, they had also gone so far as to make themselves at home by lighting both the oil-lamp and a fire in the hearth. Then, as if these two impertinances weren't enough, they had gone further and helped themselves to his ancient gramophone and his collection of violin records!

"That's my Beethoven concerto," he told himself, and added: "What a cheek!"

Count Alucard was outraged. So much so, in fact, that he felt like striding in through the door and confronting the castle-breakers, face to face and man to man. But what the Count felt like doing and what he actually did were two entirely separate things. For the Count was quite a timid man by nature. He lacked the courage to behave so boldly. Instead, he tiptoed through the snow and knocked, very gently, on the dark iron-studded big front door.

"H-h-h-h-hello?" the Count stammered, softly. "Is there anyone th-th-there?"

Naturally, there was no reply – for no one within could have heard either the gentle knock or the nervous words. The Count remained where he was, shivering from both the cold and from his sorry plight, on the Castle Alucard's icy doorstep.

"Come, come, my dear chap!" the Count murmured to himself at last. "This is no way to behave at all. 'A Transylvanian vampire's castle is his *home*', as the saying goes. What would your late father have said, if he could have seen you now? He would have been *ashamed* of you! You may not have inherited your ancestors' blood-drinking habits, but surely you are heir to a little, at least, of their courage?"

Then, summoning up all of that daring that had been handed down to him by past generations, and with his heart beating wildly inside his chest, Count Alucard took a tight hold on the rusting iron bell-pull which had hung outside the castle door for centuries, and tugged at it with all the strength that he could muster. Nervously, he listened as the bell jangled far away in the castle's below-ground kitchen. There was a pause of what must have been a minute but which seemed like an hour to the

Count, and then he heard the sound of measured footsteps approaching. Next, there was the noise of bolts being drawn, then the rattle of door-chains and, at long last, the front door creaked slowly open.

"Yes? And how may I be of service to you?" The man who had spoken was tall, rather old with greying hair and with a voice that matched his sternly disapproving face.

"You can begin by telling me," the Count began, forgetting all of his fears in the anger of the moment, "exactly who you are and what you imagine you are doing in my castle?"

"*Your* castle, sir?" said the man, raising his eyebrows in disbelief. "I'm afraid that you are under some misapprehension there. This isn't *your* castle."

"Of course it's my castle!" cried the Count, angered even further by the man's effrontery. "That is the Forest of Tolokovin, I believe?" As he spoke, the Count made a broad sweep with his right arm, taking in the far-reaching pine-trees that covered almost the entire mountain and the countryside beyond.

"I believe that to be correct, sir," said the tall man, gravely.

"In which case," continued the Count, "this must be Alucard Mountain and, by definition, this must be the Castle Alucard."

"It is indeed, sir," replied the elderly man, calmly. "I would not wish to contradict you in that particular."

"Then it *is* my castle," said the Count, pulling himself up to his full height proudly. "My name is

Alucard – as was my father's name, and his father's name before him. We have been 'Alucards' all through history. I am Count Alucard."

"If you will wait one moment, sir, I shall acquaint the master of all that you have told me," said the man.

Before the Count could answer, he found himself standing on his own front doorstep with his own front door shut firmly in his face for a second time.

"Master?" the Count puzzled to himself. "What 'master'? If there is a master of Alcuard Castle, then I am surely he . . .?"

This time though the Count did not have long to ponder over the peculiar goings-on at his family seat. Before many seconds had elapsed, the door was opened again and this time to its full extent.

"If you will be so good as to follow me, sir," said the elderly man, "I will show you into the dining-hall."

"I can find my own way into my own dining-hall, thank you very much," thought the Count but he decided that, for the moment at least, he would keep such thoughts to himself. Instead, he allowed the man to lead him into the long, vaulted-ceilinged, stone-walled hall where the tattered banners of his ancestors hung dust-laden from the minstrels gallery.

The Count took in the long refectory dining-table on which were standing two ornate silver candlesticks, both festooned with cobwebs. He saw the twenty antique dining-chairs set round the table, with each of the twenty seats padded with exquisite but faded brocade and every one of the twenty finely-carved chair-backs embellished with the letter "A" for Alucard. Lastly, and most annoyingly, he saw his own antique gramophone playing his own Beethoven recording.

Count Alucard knew and recognized every detail in the dining-hall. He had been familiar with everything inside it since he was a child. He did not recognize, however, the man sitting in the carver-chair at the head of the table who rose to greet him.

"My dear, dear fellow!" said the man, who was wearing a loud check suit, a suede waistcoat, a green shirt, a yellow tie and was sporting a monocle in his left eye. "Higgins tells me that you're Count Alucard?"

"Higgins?" said the Count.

"My butler chappie," said the monocled stranger, nodding at the elderly man who was hovering close at hand.

"Then he has told you nothing less than the truth," said the Count, nodding to acknowledge the fact, then adding: "But that leaves me at some slight disadvantage."

"I don't quite follow you, old bean?"

"You know who I am but I don't know who you are! Nor do I know what you are doing in my castle."

"Me? But I'm your cousin, don't you know."

"My cousin?" exclaimed the Count in some surprise. He had always been led to believe that he himself was the very last of the Alucards. Besides, the man did not *look* as if he belonged to the family. While the Count, in common with all of his ancestors, was tall and thin and dark, the monocled man was short and chubby with blond wavy hair. "I didn't know that I had a cousin?"

"On the English side of the family, old fruit."

"There are English Alucards?" gasped the Count.

"Not any longer, cousin," said the man, shaking his head. "Sadly, there is only one of them left. I am he. You are the last of the Transylvanian Alucards, I am the last of the English branch of the family. Allow me to introduce myself properly: I am Lord Frederick Allardyce Alucard..." He paused, extended his arms towards the Count, then added: "... I am your great-great-great-grand-cousin – several times removed – you may call me 'Freddie'."

With which, the man took two steps forward, flung his arms around the Count and embraced him warmly. As they came apart, the Count was touched to see that there were tears running down both cheeks of his long-lost relative.

Later that same night, although he was lying in the close comfort of his satin-lined coffin in the deepest of the castle's dungeons, bathed in the warm glow of light which came from the tall candles in the sconces on either side, Count Alucard was finding sleep hard to come by.

On Lord Frederick Allardyce Alucard's instructions, Higgins, the butler, had helped the Count to carry the coffin down to his favourite dungeon. It was here that the Count always spent his nights when he was in residence in Alucard Castle and, usually, he slept as soundly as any hibernating winter hedgehog.

Not on this occasion. He had too many things to think about. So much had happened in so short a time. In his head, the Count turned over the events as they had been described to him by Lord Frederick Allardyce Alucard.

Back in the late 1800s, Count Alucard's great-great-great-grandfather, Count Dracula, had travelled to England. This had not come as news to the Count. His infamous ancestor's story had been written down in the book called *Dracula* by the American writer, Bram Stoker. In that book, the author had told of how Dracula had spent some time at Whitby, the North Yorkshire fishing village, before moving on as far as London in his never-ending quest for human blood . . .

Count Alucard had known all of this. He had also known that, at about the same time as the book *Dracula* was published – and partly because of the bad publicity the publication had caused to vampires all over the world – the Transylvanian family had changed its name to "Alucard".

Relaxing in front of the roaring log fire in the ancient dining-hall as the snow began to fall again, Lord Freddie had told Count Alucard a part of the family's history which was not included in Bram Stoker's book, and which had held the Count enthralled.

During his time in Whitby, Count Dracula had met and married a simple Yorkshire country lass called Patience Thoroughgood. The marriage had lasted less than a year – by which time Count Dracula had deserted his young bride and taken himself off to the south of England in order to satisfy his vampire's appetite. He had left behind not only a wife, but also a baby son whose name was Rupert.

Rupert had grown up with the name of Dracula but not, it transpired, with his father's appetite for human blood. A hard-working and honest young fellow, he had found employment as a deck-hand on one of the many fishing smacks that put out from Whitby. Having worked hard and spent little for several years, he had put by sufficient money to take himself and his mother off to Bradford, in the West Riding of Yorkshire, where he had used what capital he had to gain himself a beginning in the woollen trade – and with some success. Then, chancing to hear that the Transylvanian Draculas had changed their name to Alucard, Rupert Dracula did the same and became Rupert Alucard.

The years passed by and business thrived. Rupert Alucard also married and he, too, had children. Rupert's eldest son, Matthew, grew up to become a wealthy mill-owner and earned himself a title, becoming Lord

Alucard and he, in turn, married and had sons and daughters.

But as the decades slipped by, the Yorkshire Alucards, like so many other Yorkshire woollen families, fell upon hard times. Not only did they lose their fortune but, one by one, they passed away and were buried in the family vault. Finally, only one Yorkshire Alucard remained – and all that Lord Frederick Allardyce Alucard possessed was his noble title and the services of Higgins, the family's loyal old retainer.

Lord Freddie had gone on to explain to Count Alucard that he had resolved to make his way to Transylvania and look up his European relatives. It was only after he had arrived in Tolokovin that he had discovered that the Transylvanian Alucards were also down to their last living member.

"And so you see, cousin," Lord Freddie had said, "when there was no one here, I had to break into the castle – where else could I have waited for your return?"

"I see," the Count had replied, staring hard into the glowing embers which were all that now remained of the blazing log fire. "And so ends your story?"

"Not quite," Lord Freddie had replied. Then, taking his gold hunter watch from out of his waistcoat pocket, he had flicked open the cover, and added: "But look how the time has flown! I think the rest can wait until the morning."

Lying sleepless in his coffin, staring up at the dungeon's ceiling, Count Alucard pondered over everything that his cousin had told him. The Count was angry with himself for not having greeted Lord Freddie in a friendlier fashion. His cousin and the butler had come all the way from England in order to meet him, and he had been little short of rude towards them.

"Never mind," Count Alucard told himself. "There will be ample opportunity to make it up to both of them in the days to come."

Then, nestling his head on his lace-edged, white silk pillow, and pondering about the ending to his cousin's story which was yet to be told, Count Alucard finally fell fast asleep . . .

3

"Are you quite sure, sir," began Higgins as he leaned over Count Alucard's shoulder, silver salver of breakfast food carefully balanced on one hand and serving-spoon and fork poised in the other, "that I cannot tempt you to partake of the grilled kidneys? They are extremely succulent."

"Take my word for it, cousin – the grilled kidneys are tip-top," said Lord Frederick Allardyce Alucard who, dressed in a red silk dressing gown, was sitting across the dining-table from the Count. "And the fried liver's done to a turn."

"No, thank you kindly, Higgins," said the Count, giving a little shiver of distaste at the sight and smell of so much cooked meat held under his nose so early in the day. Count Alucard was dressed, as always, in black suit, white starched shirt and white bow tie. "A little fresh fruit will more than suffice," he continued. "Although I would be grateful if you could replenish my glass with tomato juice – flavoured with a dash of Worcester sauce and just a touch, perhaps, of Tabasco."

"Whatever you say, sir," said the elderly butler, whisking away the loaded salver.

"Don't disappear with all that grub, Higgins," cautioned Lord Freddie, beckoning the butler

towards him. "I think I might be tempted into another pork sausage – possibly even two."

"Very good, milord."

Moments later, with the Count's glass standing brim full with spiced tomato juice and after the bowl of fresh fruit had been brought to the table, Higgins tiptoed from the dining-hall.

"Do you wish to tell me now, cousin Freddie?" asked the Count, pulling a sprig of juicy grapes off the bunch and washing them in the iced water in his finger-bowl.

"Do I wish to tell you what, old top?" asked Lord Freddie, chomping on a mouthful of crispy bacon.

"Why – whatever it was that you were referring to last night which you said could wait until this morning?"

"Ah!" Lord Frederick cleared his throat, took out his monocle, cleaned it carefully on a corner of his crisp white linen napkin, replaced it in his eye and then cleared his throat again, before continuing: "The fact of the matter, cousin, is that I thought that I might save that particular nugget of information until after we had finished breakfast."

"Oh?"

"To tell you the absolute honest truth, old fellow, I didn't wish to spoil your breakfast by being the bearer of bad tidings."

"Bad tidings?" The Count's pale face took on a solemn frown. "If you have something distasteful to impart to me, cousin Freddie, I'd far rather that you told me now and got it over with. I certainly shan't enjoy my meal worrying what might or might not be!"

In answer, Lord Frederick picked up a little polished brass handbell from the table and shook it briskly.

"You rang, milord?" said Higgins, appearing instantaneously in the doorway, as if he had been waiting outside the door for just such a summons.

"Indeed I did, Higgins. Be a good fellow and nip up to my bedroom. Fetch me down my briefcase – you'll find it by the side of my bed."

"Very good, milord."

The several minutes of silence that followed were broken by the echoing of the aged butler's slow measured footsteps retiring and returning on the wooden staircase, accompanied both ways by the sound of Lord Freddie chewing noisily on a rather gristly grilled kidney.

"I believe that this is what you were requiring, milord," said Higgins, placing a battered red-leather briefcase on the polished table in front of his master.

"Thank you, Higgins. That will be all."

Lord Freddie waited until the butler had left the dining-hall, before snapping open the briefcase. He located a long slim envelope grown yellow with the passage of many years. He opened it and took out several pages of folded parchment.

"Open it carefully, cousin," said Lord Freddie, passing the pieces of parchment to the Count. "Time has caused it to become a fragile document."

Count Alucard did as he had been told and unfolded the parchment pieces with great care. He blinked as he took in the words which had been penned in copperplate writing across the top of the first page:

LAST WILL AND TESTAMENT

"It was set down by our great-great-great-great-grandfather, cousin, back in the olden days," said Lord Freddie. "It was discovered by my great-great-great-great-grandmother, Patience Dracula, in an iron-bound trunk in her attic, long after her husband had deserted her."

"I can clearly read Count Dracula's signature," said the Count, peering at the foot of the last page of parchment. "But as for the words that come between the beginning and the end – they are so small and so tightly packed together, I can barely make out any single one of them."

"If you'll hand it back to me, old fruit, I'll read it out to you," said Lord Freddie, extending his right hand across the table while he adjusted his monocle with his left.

"There is no need for you to read it all, cousin Freddie," said the Count, passing back the pieces of parchment. "There is so much of it, I'm afraid that we should be here all morning – and I would dearly like to go outside and walk across that untrodden snow." As he spoke, the Count looked longingly out through an arched window. The snow had stopped falling during the night, leaving the castle courtyard smooth and white and invitingly free of footsteps. "In fact," the Count continued, "I would be more than happy if you would be kind enough to give me a general summary of our ancestor's last wishes – although I doubt that they will be of much interest after all these years."

"I'm not sure that you'll say that after you have heard them, cousin," said Lord Freddie, pushing his empty breakfast-plate away and drawing his side-plate and the toast-rack closer. "You see, Count Dracula's Last Will and Testament decreed that all of his possessions were to go to his son Rupert."

"I am very glad to hear it!" announced the Count. "That wicked old Count Dracula had some concern for his family after all! I imagine then that some of Rupert's inheritance went to help him to make his way in the woollen industry in Bradford?"

"Very probably," said Lord Freddie, spreading the local dairy butter generously on his Transylvanian wholemeal toast.

"But Rupert has also been dead for many, many

years. Is there any reason why you have chosen to raise the subject of his father's will after all this long time?"

"The document states that, in the event of Rupert's death, his father's effects are to be passed on to Rupert's heirs and successors."

"And they are all dead too, cousin Freddie," said Count Alucard. "Except for your good self, of course – but then, as you also told me last night, the fortune that your forebears made was all frittered away."

"That's true, alas," said Lord Frederick Allardyce Alucard. He nodded slowly, then added: "Except for Castle Alucard. I say, old bean, could I trouble you to pass me that jar of chunky marmalade?"

"I beg your pardon, Freddie?" exclaimed the Count in some dismay.

"I said: 'Might I trouble you for the marmalade?' "

"No, no, no – I mean before that?" said the Count, whose good manners compelled him automatically to push the marmalade jar in his distant relative's direction, before adding: "What was that you said about this castle?"

"Why – that it belongs to me, of course."

"Ah-Whooo-OOO-OOO . . .!"

Somewhere, in the darkest depths of the forest, a female wolf was howling for her lost mate. But if Count Alucard had heard the cry, he gave no sign of having done so.

He was standing high up on the castle's wall,

gazing out across the sea of pine trees which spread down the mountain-side, skirted the village of Tolokovin, then regrouped and stretched off again, almost as far as the Count's sharp eyes could see.

Under ordinary circumstances, on hearing the wolf-cry, Count Alucard's heart would have pumped just that little bit faster. If night were to have fallen, he would have scrambled up onto the turreted wall, spread his black cloak out wide on either side of his body, gripped its hem in outstretched hands, transformed himself into his bat-form, launched himself into the night and zapped off across the tree-tops in order to seek out and comfort the lonely wolf.

But it was not night and, even if it had been, these were no ordinary circumstances. Count Alucard's thoughts were tormented by more serious matters. He was pondering on the news which had been broken to him over breakfast by his distant relative.

"The plain and simple truth of the matter is that I am no longer master of Alucard Castle," the Count told himself sadly. "The ancient seat of the Alucards belongs to cousin Freddie. There can be no denying the fact that it was bequeathed to the English side of the family by Count Dracula himself."

Count Alucard did not doubt that fact for an instant. Even though he had not known – until he had come across Lord Frederick Allardyce Alucard in residence inside the castle – that an English branch of the family existed. Besides, the unde-niable proof was Count Dracula's parchment Last

36

Will and Testament, penned and signed by the infamous vampire himself.

Not that the Count would have doubted his cousin's word, had the will not existed. Being a totally honest man himself, Count Alucard was inclined to accept everyone he met at their face value. Besides, there were so few people in the world with so much as a kind word for the vegetarian vampire that, whenever he came across such a person, he was only too eager to show kindness in return. And no one could have been kinder towards him than his cousin, Lord Freddie.

"He has assured me that I can stay here for as long as I please," the Count reminded himself as he gazed out across the snow-covered forest that he knew so well and which he had loved since he was a child. "Apart from the fact that I won't be the owner of the castle, there is no reason on this earth why anything should change – life at Castle Alucard will go on as always, no matter who is master here . . ."

Of course it would. Castle Alucard had not changed one little bit in centuries. It had not changed during the Count's lifetime. It had not changed during his father's lifetime. It had not changed during his grandfather's lifetime. It had not changed during his grandfather's *grandfather's* lifetime. So why should it change now?

There had been times, of course, when the superstitious peasants, fearing for their lives, had stormed up the mountain-side, courageous in their numbers, bearing stakes, pitchforks and blazing torches – intent on razing the ancient castle to the ground. But there had always been an Alucard to

37

repair the damage – not only to repair, but to return the castle to its previous state exactly, beam for beam and stone for stone . . .

"No," the Count murmured softly to himself. "The old ways are the best ways and nothing ever changes here . . ."

"Sorry to interrupt your thoughts, old bean . . ."

Count Alucard, believing himself to be alone on the castle's turreted roof, jumped at the sound of Lord Freddie's voice in his ear. The Count turned to discover that his cousin had crept up the circular stone staircase and out onto the roof.

"You startled me, Freddie," said the Count.

"Didn't mean to, cousin," said Lord Freddie with an apologetic grin. "It's just that there was something that I meant to mention over breakfast and it somehow seemed to slip my mind."

"Oh? What was that?"

"I won't bother you with the details now, old chum. But 'forewarned is forearmed', as my old nanny used to say, bless her rosy cheeks. I just thought that I'd let you know, before things start to happen, that I plan to make several changes here at Alucard Castle."

"Changes?" asked the Count, aghast. "What kind of changes, cousin Freddie?"

"Wait and see," said the castle's new owner, giving the Count a secretive wink and smiling a mysterious smile.

"Hands up all those who fancy a holiday in Malta?" said Emily when the members of the Hollins family were once again seated around the coffin in the living-room. Unfortunately, Emily's was the only hand to show. "What have you both got against Malta?" she asked, crossly.

"What's Malta got to offer?" asked Albert warily.

"Listen to this," said Emily then, after clearing her throat importantly, twice, she read out aloud the description of that island printed in the travel brochure: "*Situated in the azure blue of the Mediterranean, Malta's ancient sun-kissed towns and villages have captured the hearts of travellers since time began.*"

"It *sounds* quite interesting, Mum," said Henry Hollins, allowing his own hand to creep up past his shoulder. Henry had long since given up all hope of talking his parents into going back to Transylvania, and Malta sounded as good an alternative as any other holiday resort.

The two members of the Hollins family who were holding their hands above their heads turned their eyes towards the one whose hands were both firmly rooted in his lap.

"Two against one," said Emily. "That settles it then – I'll pop into the travel agents' in the morning and book a flight."

"That's not fair!" complained Mr Hollins. "Nobody said anything about a majority vote deciding things. We're supposed to be finding somewhere that we all three want to go to."

"But there *isn't* anywhere that we all three can agree upon!" wailed Emily. "We've sat round this coffin time and time again and gone through those brochures often enough – and whenever we take a vote on somewhere, there's always one of us that doesn't want to go there." Emily paused, frowned, glared at her husband and then added: "And it's usually you, Albert, that's the difficult one to please."

"That's not fair either, Emily," replied Albert Hollins.

Fair or not though, Emily's words smacked of the truth.

The fact of the matter was that Albert Hollins was hesitant about making up his mind with regard to any proposed holiday venture. Whenever the Hollins family went on holiday, as Mr Hollins knew to his cost, unlikely things were likely to happen – usually not particularly pleasant ones.

There had been the time, for instance, when a day-trip to an English seaside town had resulted in an encounter with a real live dinosaur. On another occasion, a weekend in London had brought a meeting between Mr Hollins and a Doctor Jekyll, which had ended in Albert's being turned into the horrible hairy Mister Hyde. Then there had been the time, previously referred to when, having ventured abroad, Emily's amateur efforts at map-reading had been the cause of their straying halfway across Europe and then going through a dark forest rampant with howling wolves before arriving outside a spooky vampire castle.

"Why don't we begin again," suggested Albert, shivering at the memory of unsuccessful holidays past, "and go through the brochures, one by one, and see if we've missed anywhere out?"

"No, Albert!" said Emily, shaking her head slowly but firmly. "If we examined those brochures with a magnifying glass, we wouldn't find anywhere that we haven't considered already."

40

"It's ages yet before we go on holiday, Mum," said Henry Hollins. "Why don't we wait and see if we can get some more brochures that we haven't seen before?"

Mrs Hollins blew out her cheeks and gave a long, slow sigh. Her first foray to the travel agents had provided as many brochures as she had been able to carry. Nicholas Nickleby Close was situated at the top of a steep rise. The thought of struggling up that hill again with a bulging carrier bag full of brochures in each hand was not one that appealed to Emily at all! On the other hand, what Henry had said was right: there were several months to go before they were due to go on holiday. And, when all was said and done, Emily Hollins *did* enjoy an evening spent with her feet tucked up in an easy chair, a box of glacé fruits at her side and a pile of travel brochures to browse through.

"Why not?" said Emily.

"Jolly good!" said Albert Hollins, pleased that the awful decision had been put off until another day.

Henry Hollins said nothing but, unnoticed by his parents, he smiled a secret smile. Three months seemed like a lifetime. Three months comprised a whole twelve weeks at least. Twelve weeks contained eighty-four days. Anything might happen before eighty-four days had slipped away. Perhaps something might occur during that time that would prompt his parents into changing their minds about revisiting Transylvania. It was a slim chance but, sometimes, even the slimmest of chances came to pass . . .

"Gruuu-UUU-UUUFFF . . .!" Olga, the oldest she-wolf in the Tolokovin pack, had lifted her head, pricked her ears and given a low suspicious growl at the sound of snow shifting on a pine-tree's branches and sliding onto the forest floor.

"Easy, old girl," said Count Alucard, slipping a hand under the she-wolf's head and gently ruffling the folds of grey-white fur that hung below her jowls. "Easy, easy – nothing to fear."

Reassured at the Count's soothing tones, Olga relaxed again and allowed her head to settle back onto the soft snow cushion in the clearing.

Count Alucard had wandered deep into the forest to be alone with his thoughts. He had sat down on a fallen log in order to ponder over the "changes" at which his cousin had hinted. But the Count had not been left alone with his thoughts for very long.

Igor, an outlying patrolling guard-wolf, had been the first to come across the Count. Igor's welcoming howl had also served to bring the entire pack into the clearing. The younger wolves had been first to arrive and had slobbered and slavered around Count Alucard's legs, each one thusting its head towards his outstretched hands, jostling for his attention. The cubs came next, eagerly bounding full-bodied through snow-drifts taller than themselves, some of them too young to recognize the Count but all eager to catch up with their older brothers and sisters and cousins. The rest of the pack had padded along behind, anxious to renew the Count's acquaintance but equally keen to preserve their animal dignity.

All of which had happened some several minutes

before. Friendships had now been renewed. Greetings had been exchanged. The pack had trodden down the clearing's snow and were lying in a contented circle around the Count.

"One thing at least is certain," the Count murmured to himself as he scanned the wolves that surrounded him, "no matter what manner of changes Lord Freddie seeks to bring about inside the castle walls, the forest world will go on as always . . ."

"Crrr-aaack . . .!"

The pack stirred silently at the sudden sound. The wolves had recognized it instantly. Even little Gronya, the smallest cub in the pack, could tell the noise a twig makes when it breaks underneath a human's foot. Noses twitched, ears were pricked and heads turned for guidance towards Boris, the wise old pack-leader.

"Snnn-aaap . . .!"

The same sort of sound again, but this time closer.

Taking their lead from Boris, the wolves rose to their feet, again without a sound, then sprang off in tight formation out of the clearing and into the forest, plunging through snow-drifts and heading in the opposite direction to that from which the sounds had come.

Count Alucard was left alone with his thoughts again. But not for long. He clambered to his feet and turned in the direction of the sound of footsteps approaching through the snow. A man's voice was raised, raucously, in the chorus of an old Tolokovin folk-song of which the Count thoroughly disapproved:

> *"Zora hop-la,*
> *Zokola zarka-zarka,*
> *Zora zolka,*
> *Zokola hop-hop-HA . . .!"*

It was a song about a rabbit which was eaten by a fox which, in turn, was shot by a hunter. The Count winced and pulled a face, recognizing first the voice and then the weather-beaten face of the singer, approaching through the trees.

Emil Gruff, the woodcutter, a thick-set red-bearded man who lived alone in the heart of the forest, was on his way to chop down his day's quota of pine trees.

Count Alucard's heart seemed to sink right down into his shiny black shoes at the thought of meeting Emil Gruff. The woodcutter was never slow in making known his hatred for Count Alucard. Emil Gruff detested the Count for all kinds of reasons – but principally because of the relationship that existed between the Count and the wolves. The woodcutter's loathing for the wolf-pack was surpassed only by his loathing for the Count.

From daybreak to nightfall, from Monday to Saturday and on fifty-two weeks of every year, Emil Gruff chopped down trees – on Sundays he set wolf-traps all over the forest, but without a great deal of success. He frequently found his traps sprung, but empty. The woodcutter felt sure that some interfering busybody was tampering with his traps. He had no proof of the wretch's identity, but Count Alucard's name was at the very top of his list of suspects.

The woodcutter's suspicions were well-grounded.

Count Alucard glanced urgently around the clearing. He wondered whether to take to his heels or look for a hiding-place? He knew that if Emil Gruff were to see him, then the insults, the jibes, the jeers and the name-calling would begin. But the Count hesitated too long in making up his mind.

Emil Gruff strode into the clearing, his gleaming axe on its long shaft slung over the worn shoulder of his shabby jacket.

And then, as so often happens in real life, the totally unexpected happened.

At the same instant that Emil Gruff set eyes on Count Alucard, the woodcutter's weatherbeaten cheeks began to tremble. His mouth twitched for a second or two and then his lips settled themselves into a shape that few men had ever seen on Gruff's face.

Emil Gruff was smiling.

Emil Gruff did not smile often. Gruff himself, if asked, would have been hard put to recollect the last time when such an occurrence had taken place. Because the woodcutter smiled so infrequently, his features lacked practice at assembling themselves into the required position. It took time for Emil Gruff to smile. Had he been required to provide a scowl, Gruff could have done so in less time than it takes to wink. Scowling came naturally to Emil Gruff – smiling did not.

All the same, on that morning in the clearing, a smile did assemble itself on the woodcutter's face – even though it did not seem to suit his features and was not at all a pleasant sight.

"Count Alucard!" Gruff cried out, in a voice that was meant to match his smile. "What a wonderful surprise!"

"G-g-g-good morning, Emil Gruff!" stammered the bewildered Count.

"You should come into the forest much more often, your lordship," the woodcutter continued, his lips writhing and twitching as they strove to keep the smile in place. "We are always honoured by your noble presence."

Then, lifting his axe with his brawny right arm, Gruff swung it high above his head where its keen edge glinted in the morning sunlight as he waved his cheery goodbye to the Count. Then the woodcutter strode off again along the forest path, singing his mournful Tolokovin folk-song, the words drifting back into the clearing:

> *"Zora hop-la,*
> *Zokola zarka-zarka,*
> *Zora zolka . . ."*

Count Alucard waited until the woodcutter's song had faded into the forest and then he sank back onto the fallen log in sheer disbelief. Turning the curious encounter over in his mind, he remembered the similar greetings he had had from Eric Horowitz and Sergeant Alphonse Kropotel in Tolokovin on the previous night. Suddenly, everyone was being kind towards him.

But *why*?

Could it be possible that the pleasantries he had received from the village shopkeeper, the police sergeant and the woodcutter had been sparked off by a common factor?

But *what*?

Might it be, he also wondered, that the changed attitudes of Tolokovinites towards him could have something to do with the arrival at Castle Alucard of his English cousin?

But *how*?

Count Alucard resolved that, one way or another, he would seek out the answers to all three of these questions – and also those to several others which were already forming at the back of his mind.

4

"Mister Macintosh!" hissed Glenda Glover, the travel agent's assistant, blinking anxiously through her tinted glasses and over the top of her computer at her employer. Then, receiving no reply, she hissed at him again and more urgently than before: "Mister *Macintosh*!"

"Not just now, if you don't mind, Glenda," replied Donald Macintosh in a low cross voice and without glancing up from the pile of important-looking documents he was poring over at his desk. "Can't you see that I'm up to my eyes in work?"

Which was not strictly true. Mr Macintosh, the manager of Faraway Places, the travel agency situated in Jacob Marley Street, which was a little shopping cul-de-sac tucked away in the heart of Staplewood, was not really "up to his eyes in work". He was only pretending to be "up to his eyes in work". The wily travel agent always kept a special batch of out-of-date invoices and the previous year's travel documents on his desk which he could pretend to be examining at any time that he did not want to be disturbed – or whenever he judged that an "awkward" customer had walked into the shop. Mr Macintosh had reason to believe that such a circumstance had just arisen.

By the way, if you are sharp enough to have noticed that – and also sufficiently interested to have wondered why? – all of the thoroughfares in Staplewood appear to have been named after characters in Charles Dickens' novels, let us pause long enough from our narrative to provide the answer. It is because that eminent Victorian writer is reckoned to have once spent an entire weekend in the town. More than that, it is also believed that he even jotted down a couple of sentences for one of his books while he was waiting for the stagecoach. When a town as small as Staplewood is lucky enough to have links with such a famous person, who can blame an ambitious and proud town council for seeking to advertise the fact?

"She's back, Mr Macintosh – it's Mrs Hollins!" hissed Glenda Glover with a gulp, nodding at Emily Hollins who had entered the shop and was standing over by the revolving brochure-stand, her back towards the travel agent and his assistant.

Emily Hollins held a plastic carrier bag in one hand, bulging with the brochures she had managed to garner that afternoon, while with her free hand she added to her collection from the revolving stand.

"I *know* that she is back again, Glenda!" whispered Mr Macintosh brusquely. "I can see Mrs Hollins quite plainly, thank you very much. I'm not blind. But perhaps, if we try to pretend that Mrs Hollins *isn't* here, she'll choose her brochures and disappear into the afternoon without so much as a word."

"I doubt it, Mr Macintosh."

"I doubt it too, Glenda – but we can only hope and pray that that is what she does . . ."

49

"Good afternoon, Mr Macintosh!" said Emily Hollins who, having not heard a word of the above conversation, turned towards the travel agent with a smile before either he or his assistant had time to offer up their hopes and prayers for her hasty exit.

"Good afternoon, Mrs Hollins," said Mr Macintosh glumly. "I was only saying to Glenda the other day that we were about due for your annual visit – wasn't I, Glenda?"

"Yes, Mr Macintosh," said Glenda Glover who, not wishing to be drawn further into the conversation, leaned forward and gazed at her computer screen.

Every year, when holiday-planning time came round, Emily Hollins followed a strict routine which she had practised for years.

Firstly, Emily made her preliminary excursion round all of the town's travel agencies – as she had done some several days before – collecting her first two carrier bags' full of brochures. The brochures were then keenly perused by Albert, Henry and herself, and their contents discussed, debated and argued over around the coffin coffee table in the living-room. Secondly, Emily Hollins carried out her "mopping-up exercise" – exactly as she was doing now – and during which she paid a return visit to the Staplewood travel agents' shops, in order to pick up any brochures that she might have missed on the first occasion.

There was another golden rule that Emily stuck to every year. She always made a point of finishing her second travel-brochure run at Faraway Places. She then sought out Mr Macintosh's advice and help and left it in his hands to book the Hollins' family holiday. Emily *liked* Mr Macintosh. Mr Macintosh was always polite and patient. Mr Macintosh was Emily's favourite travel agent. Alas though, Emily was not Mr Macintosh's favourite customer.

"Why don't you sit down, Mrs Hollins?" said the travel agent with a wan smile as he beckoned Emily towards his desk.

It was not that Mr Macintosh considered Mrs Hollins an "awkward" customer in the true sense of the word. Far from it. Mrs Hollins was not hard to please or given to complaining, like *some* customers that Mr Macintosh might care to mention.

The Hollins family, for instance, did not come back from a holiday abroad demanding a rebate because their hotel (which had looked so pretty in the brochure) was only a half-completed building surrounded by scaffolding. Neither did the Hollinses return from a holiday bemoaning the fact that while they had spent a fortnight in Madeira, their luggage had passed the same two weeks in Madrid.

In some ways, the travel agent told himself, the Hollinses were perfect customers. Except . . .

The trouble with the Hollinses was that it was hard to get them to make up their minds about where they wanted to go. They had been known to dither undecided for weeks – and sometimes even months – on end. And, worst of all, so long as the Hollinses remained undecided about their holiday destination, Emily made it her business to pop into Faraway Places several times a week – sometimes even once or twice a day – to seek out Mr Macintosh's opinion and advice on the matter.

The travel agent, remembering how conversations with Mrs Hollins could twist, turn and shoot off in all kinds of curious directions without ever arriving anywhere, chewed nervously at his lower lip as he waited for her to sit down in the chair on the other side of his desk – a position she had occupied so many times before.

"Well then, Mrs Hollins – and where is it to be this time?" began Mr Macintosh brightly, in his best travel agent's voice and hopeful that this year might be unlike any one that had gone before and that the client sitting opposite him had already made her mind up. "A fortnight's sun, sand and *sangria* on the Costa Brava perhaps – or perhaps a couple of weeks Fly-Drive in the Californian sunshine, with a trip to Disneyland and a Film Studios Tour both included in the knock-down price?"

"As a matter of fact, Mr Macintosh," said Emily, perched bird-like on the edge of her chair, her handbag balanced on her lap, its handle gripped tightly in both of her gloved hands. "I've got my heart set on a trip to Egypt this year."

"Egypt – the magic of the Middle East!" enthused the travel agent, nodding his head briskly as his spirits soared. Mrs Hollins *had* arrived with her mind made up! Wonders would never cease! "A wise choice, Mrs Hollins. Egypt has so much to offer the tourist – the bazaars in Cairo, the museums, the pyramids, the Sphinx, the Temples at Luxor, trips down the Nile! Yes, I do believe that you've made an *excellent* choice!" Then, turning to his assistant, he continued: "Glenda, dear – punch Egypt up for me on your computer screen. Let's see what sort of a never-to-be-repeated bargain holiday we can offer Mrs Hollins . . ."

"No, no, no, Mr Macintosh!" broke in Mrs Hollins. "I said that *my* heart was set on a trip to Egypt. *Mr* Hollins fancies somewhere altogether different."

"Does he now?" The travel agent's heart sank. "Does he indeed? And on where, may I ask, has Mr Hollins got his heart set?"

"Blackpool."

"Blackpool," echoed Mr Macintosh gloomily.

So this year was going to be like last year and all the years that had gone before, with the Hollinses arguing over the rival merits of Cairo and Blackpool for months on end and Mrs Hollins popping into Faraway Places with a daily report on how the argument was shaping. Mr Macintosh tried to bring his flustered thoughts to order. He wondered whether it might be wiser to convince Mr Hollins that Cairo had far more to offer the wayfarer than Blackpool – or to steer Mrs Hollins' ambitions away from Cairo and round to Blackpool? As Mrs Hollins was sitting opposite him at that very moment, he chose the latter course.

"Well, Mrs Hollins," said the travel agent, "I must say that your husband does have a point. Blackpool has a great deal to commend it as a holiday venue. There's the Pleasure Beach, the Big One, the Big Wheel – and let us not forget Blackpool Tower." Mr Macintosh paused, allowed himself a little smile, and then added: "I don't think I've ever heard mention of a *Cairo* Tower."

"That's true enough, Mr Macintosh," admitted Emily. Then, with a little frown, she continued: "On the other hand, I don't think that there are any pyramids at Blackpool."

The travel agent's shoulders drooped. Mrs Hollins had got him there. Her argument was indisputable. There *were* no pyramids at Blackpool. Furthermore, as far as he was aware, it was not the intention of Blackpool Borough Council to build any pyramids – certainly not in the foreseeable future. For if Mr Macintosh's knowledge of Ancient History was anything to go by, it took a great many slaves to put up one single pyramid. Slaves were thin on the ground in Blackpool. Also, if it was Mrs Hollins' intention to pursue the argument further, there wasn't a Sphinx in Blackpool either. Nor were there any camels on Blackpool beach – despite the fact that the Blackpool sands were ideally suited to accommodate camels . . .

"I've just had a thought, Mrs Hollins," said Mr Macintosh, deciding to pursue an altogether different train of thought. "What about that boy of yours – what's he called . . .?"

"Henry," said Mrs Hollins.

"Henry," said Mr Macintosh. "How old is he now?"

54

"Twelve," said Emily proudly.

"Is he indeed? My word how time does fly!" murmured Mr Macintosh, impressed. "Well then – surely he is old enough to voice an opinion? Why not let him have the casting vote? Let Henry decide whether it's to be Blackpool or Cairo?"

"As a matter of fact, Mr Macintosh, between you and me . . ." Mrs Hollins leaned further forward on her chair and lowered her voice so that Miss Glover could not overhear. "Although he hasn't said so in as many words, I rather fancy that Henry has *his* heart set on somewhere entirely different from his father and me."

"Is that a fact?" said Mr Macintosh, trying to hide his disappointment. "And might one enquire where?"

"Transylvania."

"*Transylvania*?"

"Mmmm," went Emily, nodding her head firmly. "He has a friend who lives in a castle there – he's a vampire count."

"Good Lord above!" Mr Macintosh's eyebrows arched alarmingly and he gave a little gulp.

Cairo, Blackpool – or a Transylvanian spooky vampire's castle! Getting the Hollinses to make their minds up this year, the travel agent told himself, could prove the most difficult task he'd ever had to face.

"This is the life!" sighed Count Alucard happily to himself as he lay in his dark wood polished coffin in the castle's deepest dungeon.

His slim body tucked up snugly in his white silk

shroud, his hands behind his head, the Count was lying back on his lace-edged white satin pillow and gazing up at the small iron-barred arched window high on the dungeon wall. Not that he could see anything. It was dark outside. The new moon had slipped behind a long low bank of scudding clouds.

It was the time of night that the Count liked best of all – those few quiet hours before the dawn when the air was still and the only sound was the occasional forlorn hooting of a lonely owl from somewhere deep in the forest.

"Ter-whooo-OOOH . . .!"

"This is the life indeed!" the Count repeated to himself as he rubbed his left big toe against the inside of his coffin.

Count Alucard relished the close comfort of the casket. He could never understand why humankind preferred the wide open territories of a bed to the cosy surround of four solid coffin walls. There was nothing to aid a good night's sleep better, as far as the Count was concerned, than being enclosed on all four sides. There were no draughts for one thing – and, secondly, there was not the slightest danger of rolling over, during a bad dream, and falling off the edge of a bed onto a hard floor.

Thank goodness for coffins! The Count had been brought up from babyhood to sleep in his coffin. His father had slept in *his* coffin and so had all of the Alucards throughout Transylvanian history. And what was good enough for his forebears was good enough for the Count.

But although Count Alucard chose to spend his sleeping hours in the same manner as his ancestors, he had not also inherited their habit of taking to the

coffin during the daylight hours and then spending the nights on restless wing, cruising through the Forest of Tolokovin and the world beyond . . . . But then, why should he when he did not share his ancestors' need for the taste of human blood?

"No, my dear old thing, this is the way that life is best lived," he told himself for a third time as he shifted his thin body inside his shroud, snuggled his head of jet-black hair on the snow-white pillow and settled himself to savour fully the dark night that was still to come.

Or so he hoped . . .

Moments later, the black of night was turned into instantaneous brightest day. The light that flooded the dungeon came in through the small barred window and lit up every corner of the stone-walled cell. The brilliance was accompanied by an urgent and continuous throbbing sound which the Count recognized as coming from some kind of generator.

Someone, for some inexplicable reason, had seen fit to bathe the Castle Alucard's courtyard with electric floodlight.

Count Alucard leaped out of his coffin. If he had not been totally awake before, the cold slab-stone floor beneath his bare toes put paid to any lingering sleepiness. Edging his feet into his gold mono-grammed black velvet slippers, he shrugged on his crimson silk dressing-gown and stumbled for the door. In no time at all he was racing up the worn stone steps that led out into the courtyard.

If the light had been bright inside the dungeon, it was even brighter in the open air. Despite the fact that dawn was still some hours away, the courtyard was bustling with workmen. But the vegetarian vampire count was scarcely aware of the activity – nor of the several vans and lorries parked nearby.

His head turned upwards, still blinking at the brilliant light, Count Alucard gazed in open-mouthed astonishment at the huge sign above the turreted castle entrance which spelled out in letters fashioned out of hundreds of glowing electric-light bulbs, the two words:

VAMPIRE CASTLE

5

"Tell me, cousin," began Lord Freddie, a broad smile across his chubby face and with the reflected gleam of the hundreds of light bulbs twinkling in his monocle, "what do you think of my first attempt at bringing Castle Alucard out of the Dark Ages?"

Count Alucard, lost for words and still struggling for breath after running up the dungeon steps, could do no more than let out a gasp and shake his head in bewilderment.

"Might I offer you both a glass of celebratory bubbly, milords?" asked Higgins, stepping from the background with a silver salver which contained a bottle of chilled champagne and two gleaming goblets. Although it was not yet dawn, Higgins was as impeccably dressed as always, a dark tie neatly knotted at the neck of his crisply-ironed white wing-collared shirt and a green-baize butler's apron over his black waistcoat and pin-striped trousers.

"Higgins, you're an admirable chap!" announced Lord Freddie as he helped himself to a goblet of champagne.

"No, thank you – not for me," said the Count, finding his tongue at last. Then, turning back to his cousin, he nodded up at the illuminated sign and added: "Surely you're not seriously intending to leave that up there for all the world to see?"

"Certainly not," replied the titled English gentleman as he sipped at his champagne. He looked across at the group of workmen who were gazing up at their handiwork in self-congratulatory admiration, and continued: "Be good chaps, you fellows, and switch it off – it's serving little purpose at the moment and there is no sense in wasting electricity. Then, turning back to the Count, he said: "Shall we go indoors, cousin? It suddenly seems to have turned quite chilly. Also, I feel I owe you a word or two of explanation."

"I think that you've got a great deal of explaining to do, Freddie," Count Alucard murmured under his breath – but he was far too polite to say it loud enough to reach the ears of the castle's new owner.

Lord Frederick Allardyce Alucard, champagne goblet in hand, led the way into the castle followed by Count Alucard in dressing-gown and slippers, with Higgins bringing up the rear, balancing the silver salver holding the champagne bottle on the outstretched thumb and fingers of his right hand.

As the generator was switched off, the hundreds of light bulbs over the castle gates flickered, dimmed and then went out, plunging the Transylvanian night back into dark. Minutes later, when the vans and lorries had moved out of the courtyard and then down the winding road towards Tolokovin, in convoy, the new moon crept out at last from behind the long, low-lying bank of cloud.

"Ah-whoo-OOO-oooh . . ." howled a wolf somewhere deep in the heart of the forest.

"But the one thing that we Alucards have always *tried* to do, cousin Freddie, is to keep ourselves to ourselves," said Count Alucard firmly. "And certainly not to advertise when we're in residence here in the castle. Goodness gracious – if experience and past history have taught us anything at all, it is that the less we bother the Tolokovin folk, the less they bother us."

"That may have been true in the old days, cousin, but it certainly doesn't hold good now," replied Lord Freddie. "Times change, coz. Things move on and we must move on with them. In fact, during the short time that I've been here – and without wishing to boast – I think that I can safely say that I've managed to strike up quite a good relationship with the local peasant-folk."

Count Alucard said nothing. He waited for his cousin to continue. But the two were sitting at the breakfast table in the dining-hall, and there were scrambled eggs, crispy bacon, grilled tomatoes and shrubel-cake (a local delicacy) – all of which Lord Freddie intended to finish off before he went on with the conversation.

Count Alucard was happy to bide his time. He had a sneaking suspicion that his cousin's last words had got something to do with the curiously welcoming greetings he had received from Eric Horowitz (the shopkeeper), Alphonse Kropotel (the police sergeant), and Emil Gruff (the woodcutter) over the last few days.

"In fact," continued Lord Freddie at long last, when he had wiped his plate clean with the final morsel of shrubel-cake and swallowed every crumb, "I might even go so far as to say, cousin, that I have managed to strike up an *excellent* relationship with the local peasantry."

"Then you are to be congratulated, Freddie," said the Count. "For you have achieved something which no Alucard has ever done before. It is hard to say how many times the Tolokovin peasants have stormed up that mountain road, with sticks and staves, pitchforks and blazing torches, intent on setting fire to this castle – I myself have rebuilt several parts of it on more than one occasion."

"You can hardly blame them, cousin," said Lord Freddie with a shrug. "They are simple superstitious people. They fear the wrath of blood-drinking vampires."

"I know." Count Alucard let out a sad slow sigh. "Even though there has not been a blood-drinking vampire dwelling inside these castle walls for a great many years. Speaking for myself, I have not tasted anything more terrible than tomato juice – nor eaten anything more sinister than peach flesh – all of my life. But that has not prevented my life from being made a misery, not only by the peasants of Tolokovin, but by similarly disposed 'simple superstitious people' all around the world."

"I must say, cousin," said Lord Freddie with a sniff, "I do feel that you are getting yourself into rather a state over very little. After all, I am an 'Alucard' myself – but I can't say that I've experienced any of the problems that seem to have beset your life."

"That's probably because you don't *look* like an 'Alucard', Freddie," said the Count. "But just you take a long hard look at *me* – could anyone mistake me for anything but what I am by birth?"

Count Alucard was absolutely right. With his two pointy teeth, there could be no mistaking him for anyone except who he was – which was partly why he chose to dress like an "Alucard". But, also, he was not ashamed of his family name – and had never done anything to shame it – so why should he pretend to be anyone except himself?

Lord Frederick Allardyce Alucard, on the other hand, had not the slightest hint of a vampire's pointy tooth on either side of his mouth. While the Transylvanian vampires all shared similar distinctive features, the English side of the family, it seemed, had taken after Patience Thoroughgood, the Whitby lass whom Count Dracula had married.

"In any case, Freddie," Count Alucard continued, "I fail to see what our looks have got to do with your putting up a great illuminated sign saying 'Vampire Castle' over the castle gates at dead of night?"

"Of course – how forgetful of me!" exclaimed Lord Freddie, slapping the palm of his hand against his forehead. "I haven't told you yet, have I, about my ingenious scheme?"

"No, Freddie," said the Count unsurely. "What ingenious scheme might that be?"

"This is really going to impress you, cousin," said Lord Freddie simpering proudly. "I'm going to turn Alucard Castle into a theme park."

"A theme park?" echoed the Count incredulously.

"Mmmm – and I engaged those workmen to put the sign up in the middle of the night in order to give you a pleasant surprise."

"A *theme park*!" gasped Count Alucard for a second time.

"Vampire Park – a theme park based on blood-drinking monsters and situated right here, in Transylvania, at Alucard Castle where our ancestors, *real* vampires every one, have dwelled for centuries," enthused Lord Freddie. "And there'll be vampire rides, a vampire restaurant, a vampire souvenir shop – all the usual kind of theme park things."

"What a dreadful thought!" said Count Alucard with a little shiver.

"Do you think so?" Lord Freddie blinked through his monocle and looked quite hurt. "You do surprise me, cousin. There are folk in Tolokovin who agree with me – they consider it to be an excellent proposition. They'll make pots of money, of course, out of the tourists who come flocking here."

So *that* was why Eric Horowitz and Alphonse Kropotel had greeted him warmly, the Count told himself. His cousin had managed to befriend the Tolokovinites by appealing to the greedy side of their nature. Trust *them*! No doubt Lord Freddie had made some similar sort of proposition to Emil Gruff? A sudden chill struck at the vegetarian vampire's heart. Surely his cousin was not intending to help the woodcutter in his mad desire to rid the forest of the wolves . . . ?

"Tourists – *here*?" the Count said aloud, gloomily, echoing, his cousin's words.

Alucard Castle had always been the one place where the Count could return for peace and quiet when he wished to escape from the cares of the world – and now his cousin was proposing to over-run the castle with tourists!

"Once you've had time to mull the idea over, old chap," said Lord Freddie, "I'm sure, you'll come round to seeing things my way – especially when you hear what exciting plans I've got in store for you."

"What exciting plans are those . . .?"

But before Lord Freddie had time to explain how he intended the Count to fit into his scheme of things, the door opened and Higgins entered, nose in the air as always, carrying a handful of envelopes of all shapes and sizes.

"The postman from Tolokovin has called, milord, on his mule," announced the butler as he handed over the bundle of letters to his employer.

"Excellent!" said Lord Freddie as he thumbed through the stack of envelopes which seemed mostly to consist of business letters. "Things seem to be on the move at last with regard to Vampire Park, Higgins."

"I am delighted to hear so, milord," replied the butler gravely. "May I make so bold as to proffer the hope that the venture proves an enormous success?"

"You may indeed, Higgins—" Lord Freddie broke off as he came across an envelope which was hand-written with a blue Air Mail sticker and a British stamp. "Why, cousin – here's someone who has actually taken the trouble to sit down and write to you! Now, who on earth would do a thing like that?"

"Thank you, Freddie," said the Count as he took the letter, recognizing the handwriting instantly. "If

you'll excuse me," he added as he headed with long strides towards the door, "I would prefer to read it in private."

Sitting on the edge of his coffin, in his dungeon, Count Alucard ripped open the envelope, took out the letter and held it towards the daylight which was filtering in through the high arched window. He read the letter slowly, savouring every word:

My dear Count Alucard,

I hope that you and all of the wolves are well. I suppose that the winter snows must have melted by now in Transylvania? It is quite warm here in England. Dad has put a new garden gnome, holding up a painted lantern, underneath the rhododendron bush to celebrate the coming of spring. Mum shines your coffin with furniture wax every week and cleans the handles with silver polish. I made an egg-holder out of plastic in Design Technology at school and I would like to give it to you as a present the next time we meet. I wish I could come and visit you soon but it looks like being

*either Blackpool or Egypt for us this year. I wish I
could change myself into a bat so that we could fly
through the forest together.*

All best wishes,
Your good friend,
Henry Hollins
*PS: I painted a picture of you in Art Class and
it was chosen to be put up on the display board in
the hall.*

Count Alucard read the letter for a second time and
a tear slid down his cheek and plopped onto the
paper.

Mrs Hollins arranged two bowls of "nibbles", one
containing salt and vinegar crisps and the other
bite-size cheesy biscuits, on separate place-mats at
either end of the polished coffin. A third place-mat,
already positioned in the centre of the coffin-lid,
held three glasses and a bottle of fizzy lemonade.

Stepping back to admire her handiwork, Emily
rang a little cut-glass handbell which she kept on
the sideboard to summon the family into the living-
room. Moments later, Henry had abandoned his
homework in his bedroom and Albert Hollins had
shrugged off his gardening boots inside the back
door. Father and son faced each other from chairs
on either side of the coffin while Emily sat in pride
of place on the sofa at the coffin's head.

"Tuck in," said Emily, nodding at the "nibbles".

"Lovely grub," said Albert, helping himself to a
cheesy biscuit. "But there was no need to go to all
this trouble."

67

"It was no trouble at all," said Emily. "And I thought it would be nice to have something to munch on while we return to the thorny subject of this year's holiday plans."

"That's what I mean," said Albert Hollins. "There was no need to go to any trouble – I've been giving the matter some consideration while I've been out in the garden planting the summer bulbs. I've rather come round to the idea of a fortnight in Egypt."

"Oh," said Emily flatly. "I've been giving the matter some consideration too – and I've quite come round to fancying a couple of weeks in Blackpool."

Henry Hollins, deciding that the discussion, as usual, would probably go on for quite some time, tucked into the salt and vinegar crisps.

"Order! ORDER!" cried Alphonse Kropotel. At the same time he banged on the table with his truncheon so hard that the three glass tumblers and the carafe of water fairly bounced on the green-baize tablecloth. "We will not arrive at any decisions if we all attempt to talk at once!"

Spring was advancing towards summer. It was the warmest day of the year so far. The overhead fan in the crowded meeting hall had broken down, as it did so often, and Tolokovin tempers were beginning to fray around the edges.

Sitting at the table on the platform, on either side of Sergeant Kropotel, were the shopkeeper, Eric Horowitz, and Henri Rumboll, the Mayor of Tolokovin. The three had appointed themselves the sole members of a committee which would consider

whether the proposed theme park at Alucard Castle would be a good thing or a bad thing for the townsfolk of Tolokovin? Not one of the three, however, was open-minded on the subject.

Horowitz, who intended to turn part of his shop into a tourist bar which would sell shrubel-cake and goat's meat sandwiches to the tourists, was very much in favour of Vampire Park. As was Sergeant Kropotel, who could see himself upping his own income with tourists' tips and bribes – and by turning the spare ground at the back of the police station into a tourist car park. Henri Rumboll, who had it in mind to organize trips around the town hall charging half a grobek a head, was as keen as his two fellow committee members to see the theme park built.

There were, however, several dissenting voices in the hall that were anxious to make themselves heard.

"If you would care to put your hands up," cried Mayor Rumboll over the general hubbub, "we will listen to you each in turn!"

A dozen hands shot up and waved frantically above their owners' heads.

One of the hands belonged to Elsa Hoggel an old woman who was sitting at the very back of the hall, half-hidden in a cloud of feathers. Elsa Hoggel was plucking a goose. The old woman's hands were too gnarled for needlework and so she spent her spare time, and earned herself the occasional grobek, by plucking geese for friends and neighbours.

Goose flesh, dried and salted, was a delicacy which accompanied shrubel-cake on feast days.

"Yes, Elsa?" called Mayor Rumboll. "Where do you stand on this matter?"

"I don't stand anywhere!" snapped the old crone, not having understood the question. "In order to pluck poultry, Henri Rumboll, I am obliged to remain seated!"

"What the mayor means, Frau Hoggel," broke in Sergeant Kropotel over the sniggers from around the hall, "is what do you think should be done about Alucard Castle?"

Elsa Hoggel scowled. There was another flurry of goose feathers. In truth, the old woman had no idea what the meeting was about. She had seen the crowds flocking into the meeting hall and had followed them in order not to feel left out. She knew nothing of the plans to build a theme park. If asked, she would not have known what a theme park was. But she did know about Alucard Castle. When she was a little girl, her grandmother had told her bedtime tales by candlelight about the creepy castle and the blood-drinking monsters who had dwelled there over the centuries. Elsa Hoggel might not have held opinions about theme parks, but she had very definite ideas about what should be done to Alucard Castle.

"Destroy it!" howled Elsa. "I am an old woman – too old to struggle up that mountain road – but you able men should take pitchforks and scythes and blazing torches. Kill everything that moves inside that castle and then burn it to the ground!"

Elsa Hoggel had spoken forcefully and some of the townspeople began to murmur in agreement.

"You should be ashamed of yourselves, you young fellows!" Elsa continued, totally obscured by feathers as she plucked all the faster in her excitement. "Sitting here while that castle stands – your grandfathers must all be turning over in their graves."

"Frau Hoggel speaks the truth!" quavered an old man who, although considering himself too old to go on a vampire hunt, was eager to see one organized.

"Yes! Yes!" croaked another ancient well past the age for combat. "Arm yourselves with sticks and stones and start out now!"

The younger peasants stirred uneasily on the wooden benches. Their hearts were urging them to mount an attack on Alucard Castle, but their heads were more in favour of caution. Even so, the mood inside the meeting hall was turning towards action.

"All of this is getting us precisely nowhere!"

71

whispered Eric Horowitz to his two fellow committee members.

"I thought the idea was to make money out of Castle Alucard," muttered Henri Rumboll, "not to set it alight!"

"Order! ORDER!" shouted Sergeant Kropotel for a second time, again accompanying his words by banging his truncheon on the table and causing carafe and glasses to leap into the air. "Either this meeting will come to instant order or I'll arrest the lot of you for breach of the peace and fine everyone two grobeks each!"

The townspeople sat still and silent and waited politely for the meeting to continue in a more peaceful vein.

"That's better," growled the police sergeant. "Now then – the plain fact of the matter is that this theme park will bring prosperity to Tolokovin and put rich pickings into our pockets. And the sooner you get that into your thick skulls, the better. Vampire Park will bring tourists flocking here with bulging pockets and purses – ready to be fleeced. Why, with a theme park on that mountain, every day in Tolokovin will be like a feast day. I tell you, friends, dried salted goose flesh and goat's meat sandwiches will sell like hot shrubel-cakes. The simple question is, do you want to be rich, or don't you?"

"We want to be rich!" was the impassioned cry that rose up from the body of the hall.

"We'll take a vote," said Mayor Rumboll as he clambered to his feet. "Hands up all those who are in favour of the theme park – those not in favour, keep your hands where they are."

All of the townspeople who could see themselves

obtaining work or making a grobek or two out of Vampire Park, shot their hands up into the air, while those who could not see themselves lining their pockets kept their hands firmly rooted in their laps.

"Sergeant Kropotel," said Henri Rumboll, "you count the raised hands while you, Eric Horowitz, count those that have stayed down."

From the look of things, it was going to be very close.

"How many for?" asked Mayor Rumboll when the counting was over.

"A hundred and twenty-seven," said Alphonse Kropotel.

"And how many against?"

"A hundred and twenty-seven also," said Eric Horowitz.

At that very moment, the door creaked open and then slammed shut at the back of the hall. Every head in the room turned to see who the latecomer might be?

"I couldn't get here any sooner," announced Emil Gruff as he shifted his axe from one grubby worn coat-shoulder to another. "There were pine trees that needed fetching down in the forest. Has the vote been taken yet?"

"Yes," said Henri Rumboll solemnly. "And it is split exactly down the middle. One hundred and twenty-seven for the theme park and one hundred and twenty-seven against it."

"Then mine is the casting vote?" as he spoke, the woodcutter swung his axe down from his shoulder and rested it against his leather-trousered right leg.

"That's true, Emil," said Eric Horowitz anxiously. "Everything rests with you. It is up to you to decide whether Vampire Park is to go ahead with Tolokovin's blessing?"

The woodcutter's face twitched several times alarmingly, his mouth jerked and then his lips settled into an uneasy smile. It was the second time that month that Emil Gruff had smiled. Smiling was getting to be a habit with the woodcutter. And why not, he asked himself? For the first time in his life the fate of many people dangled in his grasp. Good! He would let them hang there for several seconds more . . .

"Well, woodcutter?" snapped Sergeant Kropotel. "Out with it, fellow! For or against?"

"All in good time," replied Gruff grumpily. "I'm thinking about it."

In fact, he wasn't giving the matter any thought at all. There was nothing for him to think about. Gruff's mind had been made up before he walked through the door. The woodcutter was hugging a secret to himself. The new master of Alucard Castle, Lord Frederick Allardyce Alucard himself, no less, had made the woodcutter a promise. A promise that no one knew about, as yet, except the woodcutter and his lordship . . .

"Come along, Gruff!" said the mayor impatiently. "You're keeping the whole of Tolokovin waiting. Are you for or against the theme park?"

"For!" As he spoke, the woodcutter raised his arm and swung his axe above his head. The axe-blade glinted in a shaft of sunlight that was streaming in through a window.

The decision had been taken. The townsfolk of Tolokovin had come down in favour of the vampire theme park. But only the barest few of those that had cast those votes had paused to consider the seriousness of the path that they had chosen. By agreeing to co-operate with Lord Freddie's plans, they had signalled an end to the tranquil way of life in the age-old sleepy village nestling in the shadow of the Transylvanian mountain.

And, once that way of life was gone, it would never return.

6

"Perhaps, my little ones, this theme park will turn out not to be such a bad thing after all."

The members of the wolf-pack that were stretched out, snoozing in the forest glade, stirred at the sound of Count Alucard's voice. Several of the older wolves yawned while Droshka, a frisky she-wolf, lifted a hind leg and scratched delicately behind an ear in search of an impertinent flea. Without exception though, the wolves turned their heads and twitched their ears in Count Alucard's direction. The Count was sitting on a tree-stump with the wolf-pack all around him. The wolves always listened when the Count spoke to them – even though they did not understand his every word.

Ilya and Lubchik, the two young wolves that the vampire nobleman had encountered on the snow-covered cart-track several months before, rose to their feet and padded inquisitively across towards the thicker undergrowth that fringed the edge of the forest. They stretched their necks, sniffed keenly, and peered into the dark beyond – as if one lesson learned was not enough and the pair were ready to lose themselves for a second time. But a warning

growl from a senior wolf brought them scurrying back into the close safety of the pack.

It was very nearly summer. The glade was thick with grass and dotted with clumps of early flowers. The afternoon was still and warm and silent, save for the occasional twittering of bird song.

The only discord to the delightful afternoon came from the direction of the castle and consisted of the clatter of sledgehammers on steel as the workmen busied themselves building the huge rollercoaster Vampire Ride which was to be the theme park's main attraction, situated on the expanse of clearing beyond the castle's gates. Alucard Castle was all of half a mile away and the noise, muffled by the stretch of forest that lay between, was not *too* unpleasant and had sparked off the Count's remark that the theme park might yet prove to be "not such a bad thing after all".

"One must take into consideration the fact that it is already providing employment for the men of Tolokovin – and that it will bring prosperity to the district too, when the tourists begin to come," the Count continued, partly to himself and partly for the benefit of the wolves who – with the exception of an over-excited cub who was whirling round and round in a vain attempt to snatch his tail between his teeth – were giving him their polite attention. "This much is certain," the Count went on as he tugged playfully at the loose folds of skin and fur under an old wolf's jowls, "the theme park will not make one jot of difference to you, my children of the night. Life here in the forest will go on exactly as it has always done: unchanging and without interruption—"

"Count Alucard! Are you at hand, by any chance?"

"Or *almost* without interruption," the Count added as a familiar voice called out from close at hand.

Count Alucard let out a little despondent sigh. He knew, without needing to look around, that he was entirely alone in the clearing. The wolves had slipped silently and speedily away at the sound of the approaching human.

"*There* you are, my lord!" said Higgins with relief – but looking hot and flustered and out-of-place in his butler's apron as he walked nervously into the clearing. "I have been searching for you for quite some time."

"And now that you have found me, my dear Higgins, how can I be of service to you?"

"No, no, no, sir! You will forgive me if I appear to contradict you – but it is *my* duty, as a manservant, to be of service to *you*."

"If it pleases you, Mr Higgins," said the Count, biting back a smile.

"Oh, it does indeed, sir. It affords me the very *greatest* pleasure. But first, I wonder if you would deem it entirely inappropriate of me were I to make so bold as to proffer you a few words of advice?"

"You may make so bold as you desire, Mr Higgins," said the Count with the smile still hovering on his lips.

"Then if you will heed my warning, milord, in future you will not venture alone so far into the forest."

"And why not pray?"

"Because, sir, it is my considered opinion . . ." at which point, the butler paused, glanced over his shoulder nervously, and then went on: " . . . I gravely fear, sir, that there may well be several wild animals lurking in its depths."

"Wild animals, Mr Higgins?" cried the Count, his thin black eyebrows shooting up in mock surprise. "Why, whatever breed of animals do you imagine might be at large in these woods?"

"I do not wish to alarm you, sir, but I have heard it mentioned that possibly wolves abound here."

"*Wolves*! Surely not?"

"So I have heard it said, milord."

"Mercy upon us, Mr Higgins!" exclaimed Count Alucard. "Then the sooner we are back in the safe confines of Castle Alucard, the better for the both of us! Will you lead the way?"

"It will be my utmost pleasure. Oh, and by the way, milord, my master wishes a word with you," murmured Higgins smarmily, throwing up his hands in mock horror.

Glancing nervously both this way and that, the butler set off along the forest path and back the way that he had come. Count Alucard followed, keeping sufficient distance between himself and the manservant for his chuckles not to be overheard.

"Ah-whooo-OOOH . . .!"

At the sound of the wolf cry, far off in the forest, the butler increased his pace along the uneven track. Watching Higgins stumbling fearfully along, startled by every twig that snapped or branch that stirred, Count Alucard was obliged to stuff his white silk handkerchief into his mouth to stop himself from laughing out loud.

"The time has come, cousin," said Lord Freddie, slipping a friendly arm around Count Alucard's slim shoulders, "for me to explain the plans I have in store for you."

"I was beginning to wonder when you might do that?"

It was late afternoon. The pair were strolling across the clearing that stretched beyond the castle gates, overshadowed by the giant-sized, half-completed metal framework of the vampire rollercoaster. There were several other partly-built entertainments in the clearing, some of them fashioned out of metal, like the rollercoaster, others made from stone. Vampire Park was beginning to take shape.

The workmen – both the engineers who were responsible for the rollercoaster and were ferried in daily from the city, and the stone masons, brick-layers and labourers who were mostly from Toloko-vin – had all finished for the day.

Count Alucard and Lord Freddie had the part-built amusement park to themselves.

"Ah-whooo-OOO-oooh . . .!" The wolf howl drifted plaintively towards them, rising and falling on the early evening breeze.

"Here's how it's going to be then, cousin," enthused Lord Freddie as he pointed across towards the castle. "Do you see the highest part of the roof?"

"I see it," said Count Alucard, shielding his eyes with one hand and squinting up at the turreted ramparts which were silhouetted by the setting sun.

"Well then, four times daily – perhaps six times when we're *very* busy – you will skedaddle across that roof on tippy-toes with your cloak flapping out behind you . . ."

"Why will I do that, Freddie?" asked Count Alu-card doubtfully.

"To entertain the tourists, of course!" snapped Lord Freddie. "They will be assembled here, where we are standing now, to watch you. The times of your performances will be printed in the pro-gramme."

"It's not going to be much of an entertainment for them is it? Watching me go across the roof on tippy-toes?"

"I haven't finished yet, cousin!" Lord Freddie,

with one eye screwed up, glowered through his monocle fiercely at Count Alucard with the other. "Do stop interrupting."

"Sorry, Freddie."

"Here's the exciting part: when you reach the highest bit, you clamber out onto that turret that sticks out, then spread your cloak out wide – like this." Lord Freddie put out his hands and mimed what he wanted the Count to do. "Then, to the amazement of all the tourists, you turn yourself into a bat, launch yourself into the air and zoom off into the forest . . ."

"Oh dear!" said Count Alucard.

"What's the matter *now*?" Lord Freddie asked impatiently.

"I'm afraid I won't be able to do that, Freddie."

"Won't be able to do it? You've got to do it. It's going to be printed in the souvenir programmes – in black and white – that you're going to do it."

"Then you must cancel the programmes, Freddie."

"It's much too late for that, cousin," snapped Lord Freddie.

"But I *can't* change myself into a bat during the hours of daylight. That's one of the inconveniences of being born a vampire. It isn't just me. It's the same with all vampire bats. One can only accomplish the transformation when night has fallen."

"But if you were to do it after dark, the tourists wouldn't be able to see you."

"No – I don't suppose they would."

"I suppose I could arrange for the castle to be floodlit . . ."

"What a splendid idea, Freddie!" exclaimed Count Alucard, quite intrigued at the prospect of displaying his bat skills in public with the illuminated ancient castle walls as a back-drop.

"On the other hand, as most of the trippers will have left the park by teatime, we must give them some performances during daylight hours," said Lord Freddie, glowering at the Count. "*Really*, cousin! I do think that it was rather remiss of you, not to have informed me of your limitations earlier."

"I'm most awfully sorry, Freddie," said the Count, spreading his pale hands wide apart, palms upwards, in apology. "But I didn't know what was expected of me."

"It's all very well being sorry, cousin – but a great deal stands or falls on this theme park venture. Some very influential chums of mine have sunk a great deal of money into Vampire Park."

"What are you going to do about the bat flights, Freddie?"

"I expect I'll think of something," replied his lordship sourly. Then, adjusting his monocle more firmly in his eye, he added: "I usually do manage to get my brain-box working." Turning his back on the Count, Lord Frederick Allardyce Alucard stormed off, with short, quick, bad-tempered strides, towards the castle gates.

Count Alucard watched as his cousin disappeared from sight into the part-built amusement park. It had occurred to the Count, during their discussion, that Lord Freddie was being just a mite unreasonable. It was not *his* fault, the Count told himself, that he was unable to turn himself into a bat in daylight. But the Count was much too well-mannered to have told Lord Freddie that he thought him unfair. After all, Lord Freddie had been kind enough to allow him to stay on at Alucard Castle for as long as he desired – even though he no longer held any rights to his ancestral home . . .

Reflecting on all of his problems, Count Alucard stood quite still, his slim shoulders drooping, and watched as the sun's last rays crept behind the rim of the mountain-top. The Count shivered. It seemed, suddenly, as if the evening had turned quite chilly.

"She's back again, Mr Macintosh!" hissed Glenda Glover, her blue eyes blinking nervously behind her glasses. "And she's brought her family with her this time!"

Donald Macintosh's face fell as he glimpsed Mrs Hollins, with her husband and son following close behind, coming through the travel agency door.

Leaning against the bookcase in Mr Macintosh's private office, was the brand-new, red and white leather bag which held his golf clubs. Donald Macintosh was proud of his golf bag. It had been a birthday present the day before from Sharon Macintosh, his loving wife. The travel agent had been intending to show off the golf bag that very morning by playing a round of golf with his friend and fellow travel agent, Gerald Higginson, of Pickwick Holidays. The arrival of the Hollins family could well put an end to that little excursion.

Attempting to get Mrs Hollins to make up her

mind was bad enough – but with *three* Hollinses to deal with, Mr Macintosh could see his chances of getting to Staplewood's golf club that morning fading by the second.

"Will you attend to Mrs Hollins' needs, Glenda?" said Mr Macintosh as he headed purposefully towards his office, hoping that its door would close behind him before he was spotted by Mrs Hollins.

No such luck.

"Good morning, Mr Macintosh!" trilled Emily.

Mr Macintosh glanced across at his assistant hopefully, but got no help from that direction.

"I'm afraid I'm rather busy, Mr Macintosh," said Glenda Glover, holding up two hands which were full of envelopes and packages. "I've got all of this morning's mail to see to."

"Come into my office, Mrs Hollins," said Donald Macintosh, turning towards Emily Hollins with a weary smile. "Bring Mr Hollins and Master Hollins in with you – we'll have a little chat about where you think you might like to go . . ."

Moments later, sitting in his chair looking across his desk, past the Hollinses who were sitting opposite him, Mr Macintosh could see his golf bag leaning against the bookcase. Closing his eyes, the travel agent imagined himself striding out across the lush green, gently rolling slopes and the well-trodden even fairways of the golf club, pulling his posh new golf bag behind him on its trolley, watched by his envious fellow club members . . .

"What we popped in to tell you, Mr Macintosh," Emily Hollins' voice broke in on the travel agent's daydreams, "is that we've decided where we want to go for our holidays this year."

Donald Macintosh sat bolt upright in his chair, his eyes opening wide in astonishment. "Hallel-ujah!" he exulted inside his head. "The Hollinses have made their minds up! Golf club here I come!" He had expected to be chair-bound for an hour at least, while Mr and Mrs Hollins discussed and pondered over the rival merits of holiday desti-nations around the world. Instead of which, they were sitting in his office with their minds made up – and with over a month to go before they were due to set off.

"I'm pleased to hear it, Mrs Hollins," the travel agent said aloud. The thing to do, he had told him-self, was to play it cool and not to show his excitement. He pressed a button on his desk which rang a bell in the outer office. "I'll just get Miss Glover to take down your details and book your flight." Glancing down at his watch, out of the corner of his eye, he could see that it was not yet ten o'clock. Whoopee! With luck and barring traffic problems, he could be wheeling his golf bag onto the first tee before a quarter to eleven. "By the by," he added, "where exactly is it that has taken all of your fancies?"

"Well, after some consideration—"

But before Emily Hollins could disclose the identity of the chosen holiday spot, the door to Mr Macintosh's office opened and Glenda Glover breezed into the room.

"I'm glad you rang for me, Mr Macintosh – I couldn't wait to show you what's turned up in this morning's post."

86

Glenda Glover raised a hand in which she was holding a tube of rolled-up paper. She released her hold on part of the tube which un-rolled itself and proved to be a colourful and intriguing holiday poster. Although it was intended mainly for the eyes of her employer, the poster also drew the attentions of Emily, Albert and Henry Hollins in Glenda's direction.

"Brilliant!" breathed Henry Hollins.

"I must say," murmured Mr Hollins, "it's certainly something a little bit different."

"Well, I'll say this much for it," announced Emily, "it's got me thinking – and I believe we should start to consider where we're going for our holiday all over again."

"It caught my eye, and no mistake," said Glenda Glover.

Mr Macintosh said nothing. A minute ago, the Hollins' minds had been made up and now, at Miss Glover's entrance, it seemed as if discussions were about to begin again. With drooping shoulders and heavy heart, the travel agent gazed dolefully at the poster which was to blame for keeping him from his round of golf.

7

In leaps and bounds, with Boris, the wily old pack-leader at their head, the wolves raced through the forest at dead of night and in close formation. Lightly brushing the pine tree trunks, crashing through clumps of bracken, hurtling over mossy logs and, occasionally, splashing through rushing mountain streams, they ran at even speed, keeping pace with the small black furry creature which fluttered through the trees ahead of them on out-stretched wing.

Count Alucard enjoyed these moonlit outings with the wolves, his friends. The wolves relished the night adventures too – above all else, they cherished their freedom. The Forests of Tolokovin were far-reaching and there was no more pleasurable way for the wolves to remind themselves of the vastness of the territories which were their natural home, than by romping through them, mile after mile, with the vegetarian vampire bat showing them the way.

"Ah-whooo-OOO-oooooh . . .!" Boris, the grizz-led leader stretched out his greying neck and howled with sheer delight.

*

"I trust that you enjoyed your night's excursion, cousin," said Lord Freddie.

About an hour had passed. Count Alucard, picking his way on bat-claws, had eased his furry body through the barred window of his cell, fluttered to the floor and then changed back into human form. He was surprised to find Lord Freddie sitting, by candlelight, on the end of the coffin, waiting for him.

Although electric light was now available throughout the castle, the Count preferred to keep his dungeon lit by the cosy gentle glow from the two big candles in the tall wrought-iron sconces, as had always been his custom.

"Very much so, Freddie," replied the Count. "What is more important though, is that I think the wolves enjoyed it as much as I did."

"Hmmmm," Lord Freddie gave a non-committal grunt. He eased himself off the coffin and then walked slowly, taking short steps, around the cell, choosing his words as carefully as he placed one foot in front of the other. "As I have said before, cousin, it's a great pity that you can't perform that bat stuff in broad daylight – it would bring the tourists flocking in."

"I know that – and, as I have said before, I am extremely sorry." The Count gave a little apologetic shrug with his slim shoulders. "But I can't help being what I am."

"True, cousin – quite true," admitted the English lord. Then, suddenly seeming to relax, he turned to the Count with a broad smile across his chubby face, his eye twinkling behind his monocle. "As it happens, I've managed to solve the problem of the day-time bat flights without having to trouble you at all."

"Oh?" said the Count, puzzled. "How have you managed to do that?"

"I don't know whether you've been out onto the clearing recently to see how the theme park is progressing?"

"Oh, yes, indeed I have, Freddie," said the Count, nodding his head enthusiastically. "I was wandering around only yesterday. It's coming along *very* well. They've almost finished building the vampire rollercoaster – and the Vampire Burger Bar looks ready to open its doors. As a matter of fact, Freddie, I've been meaning to have a word with you about the burger bar – I was wondering whether you might consider selling some Vampire *veggie* Burgers too? You see—"

"Yes, yes, yes – all in good time, cousin!" Lord Freddie said impatiently. "we can discuss the details later. What I'm asking now, cousin, is what you thought of the taut steel wire that stretches from the roof of the castle down to the theme park fence?"

"I didn't see a taut steel wire, Freddie," the Count said, puzzled.

"I didn't think you would, old top," replied Lord Freddie, smugly. "It's extremely fine and yet remarkably strong."

"And why is it there?"

"It's what the vampire's going to come down, suspended on a harness, flapping his arms, four times daily."

"Down a *wire*?" said the Count, pulling a face. "Flapping his *arms*!"

"With plastic bat wings strapped to them."

"But when I transform myself into my bat shape, Freddie, I'm less than twenty centimetres long from snout to stern. Human size, and with plastic bat wings, I shall look entirely ridiculous. I shan't look the slightest bit like *me*."

"Don't worry, cousin – you're not the one that's going to do it. I've got a stuntman chappie coming over from England."

"You're going to get someone else to pretend that he's me?" said the Count, a trifle sadly.

"His name's Butch Brannigan, he's a body-buil-der. A fine figure of a fellow. It did occur to me that you're a shade too thin and weedy. Oh, and while we're on the subject, old bean, when Butch is walk-ing around Vampire Park between the shows, he'll be introducing himself to the public as Count Alucard – and signing autographs for the kiddies and so forth. I would appreciate it if you were to keep a low profile when Butch is about. After all, cousin, we don't want to confuse the visitors with *two* Count Alucards, do we?"

"No, Freddie," said the Count in a small, crestfallen voice. The one *good* thing about the theme park, he had always told himself, was the opportunity it would give him to meet the public face-to-face – particularly the children – and prove to them that he was not the evil monster that most folk imagined him to be. "I suppose I'll manage to find somewhere to hide myself," he said sadly. "If it would please you, I could take myself off into the forest during the daylight hours and spend my time with the wolves."

"I'm afraid that won't be at all convenient, cousin," replied Lord Freddie, rather coldly. "We're both of us going to have to pull our weight if we're to make a success of Vampire Park. Besides, I've already thought of somewhere you can spend your time when the park is open – why does it always have to be *me* that has to think of everything? – and where you'll also be making yourself useful."

"Where's that, Freddie?" asked the Count, fearing the worst.

"Behind the counter in the gift shop."

"I didn't even know that there was going to be a gift shop."

"Every theme park's got a gift shop, old fruit. You'll sell Vampire Park badges; Vampire Park car stickers; Vampire Park key rings; vampire plastic teeth; joke blood – all kinds of merchandise, in fact. What do you think of this?"

Lord Freddie picked up a T-shirt which had been hidden inside the coffin and held it up for the Count's inspection. Across the front of the T-Shirt, in letters resembling dripping blood, it said:

I'VE BEEN TO
VAMPIRE PARK
AND ALL
THAT I CAME BACK WITH
WERE A BITE
AND THIS LOUSY T-SHIRT!

"Very droll," said Count Alucard – although, in truth, he considered the wording on the T-shirt to be in rather poor taste.

But what was the use of arguing. It was getting late. The Count was feeling tired. His excursion through the forest with his friends, the wolves, had been exhilarating but it had tired him – and now these latest disclosures from his English cousin had saddened and thus tired him all the more.

"Can we talk about it in the morning, Freddie?" the Count added, slipping an arm around Lord Freddie's shoulders and leading him towards the ancient iron-studded dungeon door.

It was time to say "goodnight". Count Alucard was ready for his coffin.

Some hours later, with the candles burned down and flickering in their medieval sconces, Count Alucard was still sitting up in his coffin. Dressed in his crimson silk pyjamas with the initials "C.A." embroidered in gold thread on the pocket, he was flicking listlessly through the pages of the latest issue of *The Coffin-Maker's Journal*.

The *Coffin-Maker's Journal* was the Count's favourite bedtime reading. Under normal circumstances, a few minutes spent leafing through its colourful pages (which were amply illustrated with pictures of all kinds of coffins from all over the world) were more than sufficient to put the Count in the right mood for a good night's sleep.

But not tonight.

Although he had got into his coffin quite exhausted, the Count was finding sleep hard to come by. And while his eyes were on the pages of his magazine, his thoughts were elsewhere. He was still turning over in his head the conversation he had had that night with his English cousin.

Vampire Park was almost completed. The grand opening was scheduled to take place in little over two weeks' time, but Count Alucard was not at all happy with the way things were going. He did not like the idea of having to spend his days behind the counter of the theme park's gift shop while an impostor strolled around the park – wearing a pair of plastic wings of all things! – pretending to be him.

After all, Count Alucard told himself, it wasn't his fault that he was a tall thin gangling person. His father had been exactly the same. A lank frame was part and parcel of being born an Alucard. Besides, although a vampire might not look much in the hours of daylight, it was, after all, a creature of the night. His keen bat's hearing and his wide dark wings were the envy of all nocturnal things. It was something that his cousin did not seem to understand . . .

The Count sighed, slipped his *Coffin-Maker's Journal* underneath his lace-edged pillow, snuggled down inside his shroud, closed his eyes and then finally went to sleep – wishing hard that, before very long, something really *nice* would happen to him . . .

With taut muscles standing out across their stocky chests, the bullocks tugged with all their strength at the groaning harness.

"*Heave*, Ludwig! *Pull*, Osman!" cried Ernst Tigelwurst, the carter, as he cracked his whip over the heads of his straining charges, urging them to yet greater effort.

Although spring had reluctantly given way to summer in the forest, the travelling conditions had not improved along the Transylvanian cart-track. Where the wooden wheels had previously sunk twenty centimetres and more into the oozing mud, they now struggled to rise over sun-baked earth ridges.

"It's no good," growled the carter, glancing over his shoulder at the three passengers sitting on their suitcases in the back of his cart, along with the sacks of goose grain and the tubs of tallow he was taking to Tolokovin. "You'll have to get down."

"I think he wants us to lighten his load," explained Emily Hollins to her husband and her son.

"I want you to do more than that," growled Ernst Tigelwurst. "I need you to push – or else we shall be stuck here in these cart-ruts until kingdom come."

The Hollinses exchanged rueful glances but, without a word, they scrambled over the back of the cart and lowered themselves onto the rutted, sun-baked cart-track. Mr Hollins placed a shoulder against the ancient tailboard while Emily and Henry positioned themselves on either side of Albert, placed their hands against the cart and braced their feet against the earth.

"Ready?" asked the carter.

"Whenever you give the word!" called Albert Hollins, after glancing first at Emily and then at Henry who both nodded their assent.

"Then – *heave*, Ludwig! *Pull*, Osman!" cried Ernst Tigelwurst at his bullocks, and: "*Push*, passengers!" he called over his shoulders to the Hollins family.

Ludwig, Osman, Emily, Albert and Henry, strove with all of their concerted might and, gradually, the cart wheels rose and fell over one cart-rut hurdle after another.

"Well done!" shouted the carter as he cracked his whip over the bullocks' heads. "But don't stop now – we've another kilometre at least to travel before we even catch a glimpse of Tolokovin!"

"You can contradict me if you like," muttered Albert Hollins to his wife and son, keeping his voice down low in order that the carter would not over-hear him, "but, if you want *my* opinion, this is a poor beginning to our holiday."

As they heaved, and strained, and sweated under the Transylvanian hot summer sun, neither Emily

97

nor Henry Hollins felt disposed to argue with Albert's words.

A month and more before, when they had stood in Faraway Places, in Mr Macintosh's office, a holiday in Transylvania had seemed an excellent proposition. The poster, which Glenda Glover had held up in front of them, had hinted at something in prospect for all three. Albert Hollins had been excited at the thought of visiting Vampire Park. Emily Hollins had been drawn to the idea of spending two weeks in the age-old village of Tolokovin where – according to the brochure which had accompanied the poster – "time had stood still". Henry Hollins had been overjoyed at the opportunity of being reunited with his old chum, Count Alucard – but had not mentioned this to his parents.

The Hollinses had been to Transylvania once before. But their previous visit, during a European camping holiday, had been unintentional. Involving *real* blood-drinking vampires, howling wolves and vengeful peasants, that trip was now little more than a bad dream. They had managed, almost, to put it out of their heads and certainly did not connect it with the inviting scene on the travel poster. Henry, on the other hand, had recognized Alucard Castle instantly – but had deemed it wise not to mention the fact.

Their flight had been entirely uneventful. They had been served with a meal on a tray which had consisted of a little prawn-salad starter, cottage pie and peas, and lemon cheesecake for dessert. The coach journey from the airport to the city had been entirely pleasant – there had been a pretty Transylvanian tourist guide, in national costume, to point out the sights *en route*. It was at the point when they had been transferred from coach to bullock-cart – and had also discovered that they were the only three holidaymakers on the coach going on the Tolokovin package deal – that Albert and Emily Hollins had begun to wonder whether they might have erred in their choice of holiday?

Now, on the lonely forest track, as they puffed, grunted and strained their backs against the rough-hewn tailboard of Ernst Tigelwurst's cart, neither Emily nor Albert had the slighest doubt that either Blackpool or Egypt – or even Timbuktu – would have suited them much better.

Henry Hollins, on the other hand, had no such negative feelings. Pushing hard with both of his hands against the bullock-cart, his heart surged with joy as the cart-wheels lurched over one minor obstacle after another – every cart-rut successfully negotiated, he told himself, was one cart-rut nearer to Count Alucard.

He had not written to tell his friend he was coming to Transylvania for two separate reasons. It did not do, for one thing, in the Hollins household, to consider any holiday a certainty until you were actually on your way – and Henry would have hated to disappoint the Count. More important though, he was looking forward to surprising his friend. He could not wait to see the look of delight on Count Alucard's face when he came face-to-face with him at the castle . . .

"But, Freddie, you can't do that!" the Count

exclaimed as his thin black eyebrows rose with dismay and, simultaneously, his mouth dropped open in horror.

It was the day before the grand opening of Vampire Park was due to take place. Count Alucard and his English cousin were taking a late-afternoon stroll around the theme park where the workmen were busily attending to last-minute details. A touch of paint was being applied here; a piece of bunting was being hung there – several workers were wandering around the rides and stalls, their eyes glued to the ground, picking up any remaining pieces of litter. Everything was spick-and-span. Earlier that afternoon, the Count and Lord Freddie had tasted excitement to the full when they had been whirled around the park, as "guinea-pigs" on the very first test-outing of the thrill-a-second Vampire Ride. Having recovered their equilibrium, they had now arrived at a gate set on the park's perimeter fence where a thick-set Tolokovin workman was hammering into the ground a newly-painted sign, which read:

Shiver, Shake & Squirm With Fear!
This Way To
THE TOMB OF THE VAMPIRES
Enter If You Dare
Admission: 2 Grobeks
Children: Half price

It was this sign that had caused Count Alucard such distress.

"I'm extremely sorry, old bean," replied Lord

Freddie, in answer to the Count's protestation. "But I'm very much afraid that I've done it."

"Then I'm afraid that you must undo it, Freddie. Aren't you aware of the dangers that lie beyond that gate?"

At the other side of the fence, through the gate, there was a path which led to the edge of the clearing. At the end of the path, close by the fringe of the forest, lay the underground burial chamber of all Count Alucard's ancestors. Blood-drinking vampires every one, they had suffered the fate of all such monsters – they had been killed by having a wooden stake impaled in their hearts. Their skeletons now lay inside their coffins, the wooden stakes still transfixed in their bones, within the vaulted walls of the subterranean chamber. It was this last resting-place of vampires that Lord Frederick Allardyce Alucard intended to open to the tourists at Vampire Park. The very thought of such a rash proposition both outraged and horrified Count Alucard.

"But, Freddie!" Count Alucard continued anxiously. "Aren't you aware of what would happen if those wooden stakes were to be removed? Our blood-drinking ancestors would return to life! I do wish that you had consulted me before you even considered this deed – I could have warned you against the dangers."

"If I had consulted you, cousin, you would have reacted exactly as you are reacting now – in a totally negative fashion!" snapped Lord Frederick squinting disagreeably at the Count through his monocle. "I happen to consider that our ancestors' tomb will prove one of the theme park's best little money-

101

spinners. If I had listened to *you*, we would never have got it off the ground. Which is exactly why I didn't tell you first."

"But if our monster forebears were to come back to life – consider how awful that would be in a theme park full of children!"

"Oh – fiddlesticks to 'if', old top!" Lord Freddie replied airily. "Who cares about 'if'? Why worry about something that might never happen? Besides, those skeletons have been a-mouldering in their coffins for goodness know how long. They *can't* come back to life. I don't believe in ancient super-stitions. We might be in Transylvania, old bean, but we're not living in the Dark Ages."

Count Alucard was stunned and momentarily lost for words. But what use were words? When his English cousin set his mind on something, he was too stubborn to listen to reason. All the same, it did occur to the Count that he himself had had first-hand experience of the bones of his ancestors being brought back to living human form – and then zap-ping around the night sky and causing no end of problems.[1] But before he could begin to tell Lord Frederick about this past experience, their conver-sation was interrupted.

"If I might crave your indulgence, milord?"

Lord Frederick and Count Alucard both turned at the sound of Higgins' voice to discover that the butler had approached in company with a stocky, broad-chested stranger whose bulging muscles threatened to burst the seams of his clothing. Count Alucard could have guessed the newcomer's

[1] *The Last Vampire*

102

identity, but he had no need to do so – it was printed in big red letters across the front of the man's white T-shirt:

BUTCH BRANNIGAN
Daredevil Stuntman
The *very* best!

"Ah – Mr Brannigan! I don't believe you've met my Transylvanian cousin yet?" said Lord Freddie. Then, turning to Count Alucard, he continued: "This is the chappie who's going to do his stuff on your behalf, cousin – Butch Brannigan, the famous stuntman."

"The *very* best, your lordship," said Butch Brannigan with a cocky grin, quoting the words that were on his T-shirt. Then, grabbing Count Alucard's slim right hand in his own massive fist, he squeezed it so hard that it brought tears to the vampire's eyes. "Glad to meet you, sport!" he bellowed.

"I am delighted to make your acquaintance too, Mr Brannigan," said Count Alucard when the pain had eased. He tried to make his voice sound pleasant, but it was difficult to feel warm towards the man who had been hired to take his place – and who looked so unsuitable for the post. "I hope that your stay at Alucard Castle proves enjoyable – and that your accommodation is comfortable?"

The stuntman had been granted sole use of the Count's own favourite room: the castle's library which contained shelf after shelf of leather-bound volumes concerning the history of the Alucards through several centuries.

"Spot on!" bellowed Butch Brannigan. "And it's

going to be just like home – once I get those
mouldy old books out and my body-building
apparatus spread around the room." Butch Brannigan paused, looked Count Alucard up and down,
frowned, and then added: "You must come up one
evening and we'll pump some iron together – it'll
put some muscles on that weedy frame of yours."

Then, with a guffaw, he thumped the Count very
hard between the shoulder-blades for good
measure, knocking all the breath out of the poor
vegetarian Vampire's body.

Several moments later, when Count Alucard was
breathing easily again, he watched as Higgins led
Lord Freddie and Butch Brannigan back towards
the castle. It had been decided that they would
crack open a bottle of champagne, toast each

other's health and also raise their glasses to the success of Vampire Park.

Count Alucard had turned down the invitation to join them. He preferred to watch the sun sink behind the mountains and to savour what was left of the peace and quiet of the evening air. From the next day onwards, the Count had told himself, when Vampire Park was a going concern, there would be little peace and quiet left to savour . . .

"Ah-whooo-OOO-oooh . . ." A wolf howled somewhere deep in the forest.

8

Although the peeling, green-painted door was only partly open, the Hollinses could see that the old woman, who was peering out at them suspiciously, was dressed entirely in black: black skirt, black blouse, black apron, black stockings and black, very worn shoes. She had a wrinkled face, sharp piercing eyes, rosy cheeks, and there were any number of small white feathers nestling in her grey hair.

"Are you Frau Hoggel?" asked Albert Hollins.

"Who wants to know?" growled the old woman.

"We're the Hollins family," said Emily.

Elsa Hoggel looked all three of the Hollinses up and down in turn, then turned her gaze on the three suitcases at their feet for several seconds before deciding to open the door just wide enough for them to enter.

"You'd better come inside," said Elsa Hoggel.

Albert Hollins picked up the two largest suitcases and led the way. He had to bend his head in order to step through the low doorway. Henry Hollins picked up the third suitcase and followed his mother through the door into the tiny living-room which opened directly onto the cobbled street.

"You must excuse the mess," said Elsa Hoggel,

nodding first at the white feathers which were lit-
tered over the floor and furniture, then indicating
the big bird's naked carcase which was hanging
from a hook in the white-washed fireplace.
"Tomorrow is a feast day – I've just been plucking a
goose."

Albert and Henry Hollins lowered the luggage
onto the stone-slab floor and stood with Emily,
quite still for several moments, taking in their oak-
beamed, low-ceilinged surroundings.

Elsa Hoggel's living-room fitted exactly the
wording in the Faraway Places travel brochure:
time really did appear to have "stood quite still"
there.

There was an ancient pot-bellied stove in the
fireplace, belching occasional small clouds of
smoke. Above the fireplace was a mantelpiece along
which were ranged all manner of pottery bric-a-
brac and a dozen and more small frames – some
wood, some silver – containing photographs, all
yellowing with age, of bearded, bowler-hatted,
stern-faced men and lace-capped, prim-faced
women, from a time long gone. There was a mangy
ginger cat, stretched out on a rush mat in front of
the stove, which paid scant attention to a wooden
cuckoo as it creaked out of a carved clock over
the mantelpiece, "Cucked" mournfully five times
without "Oo-ing" once and then, its duties over for
another hour, creaked back inside the clock again.
There was a large table with a well-scrubbed top,
around which were ranged six large, unmatching
but equally uncomfortable-looking wooden chairs.
There was a rough-hewn sideboard on which were
standing a bowl of green figs, a pottery statuette of

107

a young girl holding two cherries poised above her open mouth and still more framed ancient photographs of Elsa Hoggel's relatives who had all, presumably, long since taken up residence in the cemetery.

There was a partly open door beyond which lay the kitchen, similarly simply furnished, and there must have been another door opening onto the back-yard for, as the Hollins family watched, an old brown hen strutted into the living-room in search of titbits then, spotting the cat, turned instantly on its claws and strutted out again.

Emily Hollins, unused to the sight of a fowl having the run of a home, cleared her throat loudly, twice, by way of showing her disapproval.

When Mr Macintosh had explained to the Hollinses, some weeks before, that there were neither hotels nor registered boarding houses in Tolokovin – but that one of the joys of that particular package holiday would be the opportunity to share the simple, honest-to-goodness way of life inside a Tolokovin home – they had taken the travel agent at his word.

Now, as they contemplated sharing Elsa Hoggel's lifestyle for the next fortnight, they were beginning to have second thoughts.

"Have you eaten?" asked the old peasant woman, perhaps guessing at their misgivings.

"Not since the meal they gave us on the aeroplane," said Emily quickly.

The in-flight meals – even the flight itself – seemed to belong to a long time ago, like something from another world almost. Since when, they had spent several hours helping Ernst Tigelwurst's bullocks progress his cart along the rutted cart-track. Then, having unloaded their suitcases in the market-place, the carter had given them brusque directions as to the whereabouts of Elsa Hoggel's house, and driven off. They had then wasted another half hour at least in knocking fruitlessly on the doors of empty houses or following misleading instructions.

However, here they were at last – and with a meal in the offing, it would seem.

"I've got dried, salted goose flesh in the larder!" announced the old peasant-woman.

"*Very* nice," said Emily Hollins, doing her best to sound enthusiastic.

"And there's shrubel-cake to follow."

"What a treat!" said Emily. Then, as Elsa Hoggel scuttled into the kitchen, followed at a more leisurely pace by the ginger cat, Mrs Hollins turned to her husband and whispered: "What's shrubel-cake?"

"Lord only knows," replied Albert Hollins with a sigh. "Have you got any thoughts on the subject, Henry?"

Henry Hollins raised his eyebrows, shrugged his shoulders and shook his head. The ingredients of shrubel-cake were a mystery to him, too.

Despite the fact that they had suffered a hectic day, Albert and Emily Hollins had trouble in falling asleep on their first night in Tolokovin.

Firstly, the bed was not to their liking. Because she had paying visitors, Elsa Hoggel had moved out of her own front bedroom and Mr and Mrs Hollins

110

had been granted use of the old peasant woman's own brass bed. The bed itself was not to blame. It was the lumpy mattress, stuffed with goose feathers, that provided them with a problem. Like the bed, the mattress had been in Elsa Hoggel's family for several generations. Over the years, the mattress had settled itself into a shape that satisfied the old peasant woman's bony frame and it refused to yield itself into another. Both Emily and Albert tossed and turned on its many bumps and hollows without managing to find comfortable positions.

Next, there was a picture hanging over the big brass bed which Emily and Albert found disturbing. It was a framed painting of Saint Unfortunato, the patron saint of Tolokovin. Unfortunato had been a medieval fighting man who had had all of his arms and legs chopped off by invading hordes. The framed picture showed the poor Unfortunato without these limbs and with blood gushing out of the four holes where the limbs had been. Although the bedroom was in total darkness, neither Emily nor Albert could rid their mind of the picture's gloomy presence. They did not find it conducive to sleep.

Lastly, neither dried, salted goose meat nor shrubel-cake had proved advisable fare for a late-night snack.

"Pardon me!" said Albert Hollins as his stomach rumbled for the umpteenth time.

"Whoops-a-daisy!" whispered Emily, in some slight embarrassment, as her tummy noisily echoed Albert's.

Elsa Hoggel, curled up uncomfortably on the straw that was scattered over the wooden-boarded floor of the hen hut, could not sleep either.

The old peasant woman did not normally spend the hours of darkness with her back-yard feathered friends. But having let two bedrooms to the English tourists when, if truth be told, "two" was the sum total of bedrooms in the house, Frau Hoggel had little choice in the matter. Not that Elsa was complaining. Being as eager as all of her fellow villagers to make as much money as possible out of the expected flood of foreign tourists, Elsa was happy to spend the occasional night with her hens.

It was not the uncomfortableness of her surroundings that was keeping the old peasant woman awake that night. It was greedily counting, over and over in her head, the number of grobeks she was going to put into her purse.

Henry Hollins, lying underneath the rough blankets on the iron-framed single bed in the tiny whitewashed bedroom at the back of Elsa Hoggel's home, was also wide awake.

Henry was far too excited to sleep. His thoughts were on the following day when, as he already knew, the theme park at Alucard Castle was to be officially opened. The Hollins family's package holiday was geared to take in that colourful event. Henry Hollins had already reasoned to himself that he would not have the opportunity to speak to Count Alucard until well on in the afternoon. The Count would be far too busy attending to official matters and important people to be able to spare any time for Henry. But, once the opening ceremony had been completed, Henry Hollins intended to find a way of gaining Count Alucard's attention. One way or another, the boy assured himself, he and the Count would meet and greet each other like the old friends they truly were . . .

"It will be like old times all over again!" Henry Hollins happily informed himself. Then, nestling his head on the goose-feather-stuffed pillow, he closed his eyes and looked forward to the blissful moment when, after all this time, he would again set eyes upon the Count.

"By the by, old fruit," began Lord Frederick Allardyce Alucard, tucking into his usual big fried English breakfast, "it might be a good idea if you were to keep out of the way during the opening ceremony this afternoon."

"I beg your pardon!" gasped Count Alucard, hardly able to believe his ears.

There was a carnival air abroad outside in Vampire Park that morning. Count Alucard, always an early riser, had been for a stroll around the theme park before coming into the dining-hall.

Some of the workmen were busily employed with last minute adjustments to the rides and sideshows. Others were attaching flags of all nations to the platform which had been built to accommodate the official visitors to the opening ceremony. Still more were attending to those last little details which would ensure that the occasion was an outstanding success. The Tolokovin village bandsmen, togged out in their best uniforms and engaged to

113

play throughout the proceedings, were standing around in twos and threes, ready for a final rehearsal.

There was little that life had to offer, the Count had told himself, quite so delightful as being out-doors on a summer afternoon, licking a strawberry ice-cream, perhaps, and listening to the breezy music of a uniformed brass band . . .

Already resigned to the fact that he would be spending his working days behind the gift shop counter, Count Alucard had never doubted for an instant that he would not be allowed to attend the theme park's grand opening ceremony. Even if it might be considered foolish to have *two* "Count Alucards" (himself and the stuntman), sitting up on the platform, the Count could see no reason why he shouldn't be allowed to lose himself as a humble bystander in the general throng, where he might listen to the band. But even that small pleasure, it seemed, was to be denied him.

"But, Freddie—"

"His lordship's right," broke in Butch Branni-gan, spearing a plump pork sausage from a silver salver and then also capturing two rashers of crispy bacon with the same swift stroke of his fork. "Your best place this afternoon, Count," continued the stuntman with a chuckle, "is tucked away behind the vampire plastic teeth and the bottles of joke blood."

Count Alucard did not reply. He took a sip of his tomato juice and munched quietly on his breakfast grapefruit while, at the same time, he struck a secret wager with himself as to which one of his two companions would manage to wolf down the most

114

number of sausages. He had decided to drop the subject of that afternoon's opening ceremony. What was the point of arguing? Lord Freddie was now master of Alucard Castle – and his word was law within the boundaries of the Alucard estate . . . Besides, there was another question nagging at the back of his mind – and one to which he sought an answer.

"Freddie?" said the Count, as he mentally added another sausage to the total of the four his cousin had already consumed.

"Mmmm?" mumbled Lord Frederick through a mouthful of half-chewed sausage number five. "What's the problem now, old sport?"

"I thought that the workmen had finished all the construction tasks several days ago?"

"So they did, cousin. Bang on schedule. I will say this much for the local peasants: they may not be the hardest workers in the world, but offer them a couple of extra grobeks as an incentive and they really do knuckle down to the job. Why do you ask?"

"I noticed something rather strange when I was out on my early morning stroll." The Count frowned and his long, slim fingers fluttered in slight agitation as he continued: "I'm sure I heard the sounds of hammering and sawing from somewhere close by in the forest?"

"Ah!" Lord Freddie paused and squinted through his monocle for a couple of seconds at the remaining half of the sausage that was poised on his fork, and then went on: "There was a little task I set some of the carpenters, now that you ask – but it's nothing you need concern yourself with, old fruit."

Again, Count Alucard kept his silence. His cousin's answer had perturbed him slightly. It had occurred to the Count on previous occasions that whenever his cousin mentioned something that "need not concern his attention", it always proved to be something that concerned him *very* much indeed. There had, for instance, been that foolish business of opening his ancestors' tomb to the general public. Also, he felt sure that he had just noticed a secretive sort of glance exchanged between Lord Freddie and Butch Brannigan. It was all most disconcerting, Count Alucard told himself . . .

"Ah - whoo - whoo - WHOOoooooh . . .!" The far-off yelping of a young wolf hung on the morning air and then petered out as it drifted in through the dining-hall's open arched window.

Deep in the very heart of the forest, Emil Gruff swung his axe at the undergrowth close by his feet and then, screwing up his eyes, peered into the trees. Although the sun was already climbing high into the clear blue sky, its rays failed to filter through the tight network of pine branches. The woodcutter had difficulty in seeing the shadowy figure of the peasant, clutching a pitchfork, on his left-hand side, even though the man was no more than twenty metres or so away. Similarly, glancing to his right, Emil Gruff could only just make out another peasant positioned the same distance away as the first, and clutching a glinting scythe. The woodcutter knew, even though he could not see them, that there were some fifty or so more Toloko-

116

vinites, all bearing makeshift weapons, ranged on either side of him at equal distances. The line stretched right across the belt of forest which continued, up the mountain-side towards the theme park and the Castle Alucard.

"Are you ready?" cried the woodcutter.

"Aye! Ready!" came the reply – first from those nearest to him and then repeated all along the line.

"Then forward! But slowly!" commanded Gruff.

"Forward – slowly!" echoed all along the rank.

Holding the same distance between each man, the line of peasants edged forward through the shadowy trees, moving slowly up the mountain and beating at the undergrowth as they went, with hoe, and scythe, and pitchfork – or whatever implement they had to hand.

"Ah-whooo-oooOOOH . . .!" A young female wolf, Relka, who had been hiding in the undergrowth ahead, puzzled by the peasants' presence, now broke cover as the advancing line drew closer. Turning sharply, the wolf sped off, loping through the gently rising wooded slopes to give warning to the rest of the pack.

"Ah-whooo-oooOOOH . . .!" Relka howled again, throwing back her head and opening wide her jaws as she increased her speed and raced with even stride towards the clearing where the remainder of the pack were resting.

Without pausing once, without a change in pace and without exchanging a single word, the line of peasants, led by Emil Gruff, pressed onward through the forest, moving slowly upwards, and in the direction of the theme park which was situated some kilometre and a half ahead of them.

There was the sudden sound of beating wings as a flock of birds, disturbed by the arrival of the line of men, took instant flight from the branches of the pine tree in which they had been gathered, rose into the clear blue sky and hovered over the tree-tops. At ground level, apart from the occasional scuttling rabbit – and one solitary startled stag which, because of its sheer size, succeeded in breaking through the advancing peasant line – the only wild-life to be found between Vampire Park's perimeter fence and the woodcutter's men were the wolves.

Knowing that the fate of the entire wolf-pack lay in his hands, Emil Gruff allowed his mouth to twitch several times and then settle into a gloating smirk.

"I swear, upon the grave of my grandmother," the woodcutter growled to himself, "that the wretched beasts shall never trouble me again!"

9

"My goodness me!" murmured Emily Hollins to Albert and Henry as they turned the corner that led them into Tolokovin's market square. "This is a bit more like it!"

"I'll say it is!" said Albert Hollins enthusiastically. "What do you think, Henry?"

"It's great, Dad," agreed Henry Hollins.

There was an air of jubilation in the age-old cobbled square. Several long lengths of bunting, left over from the theme park's decorations, had been hung from some of the higher buildings and then joined together, at their other ends, on top of the statue of Saint Unfortunato, which graced the middle of the square.

The day had been declared a public holiday by the Mayor, Henri Rumboll, and the market square was thronged with folk all eagerly awaiting the transport which was to convey them up the mountain road to Vampire Park for the official opening ceremony.

While most of the local menfolk were absent, being employed as either operators or engineers or stall attendants at the theme park – or in secretly assisting Emil Gruff to carry out his task in the forest – the women and children of Tolokovin were

all assembled in their Sunday best. The women were dressed in colourful dirndl skirts and hand-embroidered blouses, while the children wore newly-laundered, crisply-ironed smocks and frocks.

An enterprising peasant had set up a trestle table and was selling goat's milk, shrubel-cake and little plastic statues of Saint Unfortunato.

Another go-ahead peasant had hastily erected a makeshift barbecue from which he was dispensing goat-burgers and strips of dried goose-flesh grilled on sticks.

And while the theme park's opening had not attracted quite so many foreign visitors as Lord Freddie might have hoped, the Hollinses were not the only tourists gathered in the market square.

There was a German family, the Grunwalds, from Düsseldorf, which consisted of the father, Hans, the mother, Frieda, and Greta, their daughter who was about the same age as Henry Hollins. Also, there was an old couple from Milan, Franco and Rosa Granelli, who had won their Transylvanian holiday in an Italian television phone-in quiz. Lastly, there was a shy young Welsh pair, Ivor and

120

Bronwyn Williams, who had been married only the day before in Glamorgan, and had chosen the Vampire Park package holiday for their honeymoon trip.

These last two, having made the Hollins' acquaintance in the market square, shyly informed Emily that they had arrived in Tolokovin in the early hours of that same morning and, as no accommodation seemed to be available for them, they had spent what was left of their wedding-night curled up on some sacks of chicken feed in the store-room of Eric Horowitz's village shop.

"Oh, dear me!" Emily murmured in concern, when this information was relayed to her. "What an awful start to your married life!"

"Oh, it wasn't *too* bad," the newly-wed Mrs Williams replied, glancing down shyly at the cobblestones and slipping her fingers into her bridegroom's hand. "There was a skylight right above our heads and we could see the moon and any number of stars."

"And I've managed to sort out the mix-up over our accommodation this morning," announced Ivor Williams, proudly. "We're staying with a very nice old couple called Karl and Eva Fassbinder."

"We've got their *whole* attic to ourselves," enthused Bronwyn Williams. "It's got a wooden floor with a big rush carpet, ever such pretty wallpaper, a wooden wardrobe *and* a chest-of-drawers." The young Welsh bride paused, pulled a face, and then continued. "There was only one thing wrong with it: there was this *horrible* picture hanging over the bed . . ."

"Say no more," broke in Albert Hollins. "I'll bet

it's a painting of a chap with blood gushing out of the holes where his arms and legs used to be?"

"However did you know that?" gasped Bronwyn Williams.

"Easy-peasy," said Emily with a wry smile. "We've got one in our bedroom as well."

"It's Saint Unfortunato – he's the patron saint of Tolokovin," explained Henry Hollins who, because of his long friendship with Count Alucard, had learned something of Tolokovin's history. "That's him over there," he continued, pointing to the statue in the centre of the cobbled square which was now covered in bunting. "Before he had his arms and legs chopped off," Henry added.

"Well! Who'd have guessed it!" exclaimed Bronwyn Williams, raising her eyebrows in surprise as she glanced over at the martyr's statue, complete in every limb. "Anyway, we've taken the picture down off the wall and hidden it behind the chest-of-drawers – so it doesn't really bother us."

"What a good idea!" said Emily, digging Albert in the ribs. "We'll do the same tonight. I don't know why you didn't think of it."

Before Mr Hollins could apologize for his short-comings, the conversation was brought to a halt by the arrival of the transport in the market square.

The procession was led by Tolokovin's shiny black hearse, the ornate silver baubles on its roof extra-specially polished for the occasion and glistening in the sunlight. The two magnificent coal-black horses that pranced skittishly between the hearse's shafts had elegant purple plumes attached to their harness, which bobbed and swayed as they arched their necks. The undertaker, Klaus Fogelmann, was sitting up on the driving-seat wearing his usual melancholy expression, but with a gaudy yellow sash tied round his black top hat. In place of a coffin, the hearse had been fitted out with four matching wooden chairs which had been fastened onto the floor.

Behind the hearse came Ernst Tigelwurst's bullock-cart. There were a couple of benches on the back for the comfort and convenience of passengers. The bullocks' horns had been garlanded with wild flowers to suit the festive occasion. Then, following the bullock-cart, there were any number of horse-drawn carts, of all shapes and sizes, which had been summoned into service from farms for miles around, with their owners, also in their Sunday best, gravely holding the reins.

The line of curiously contrasting vehicles came to a ragged halt along one side of the cobbled square.

"Stand back! Stand back!" cried Police Sergeant Alphonse Kropotel, his medals jangling on his chest as he scurried along the line of carts, gesturing at the crowds, who were pressing eagerly forward, to step back. "Stand back, everyone, until I give the word!"

The reason for the delay was suddenly made clear as Mayor Henri Rumboll, suitably dark-suited, top-hatted, and with his broad green-and-gold sash of office hanging over one shoulder and across his body, strode importantly out of the village hall. Eric Horowitz, shopkeeper and village-clerk, strutted along at the mayor's side, wearing a similar but slightly smaller sash across his own ample stomach. These two important village

123

dignitaries were followed by their equally important wives.

As the crowd swayed back to allow them right of
way, Sergeant Kropotel opened the doors at the
back of the hearse and, not without difficulty and
some loss of dignity, the four important persons
scrambled inside.

"All aboard!" shouted Sergeant Alphonse Kropotel, once the doors of the hearse had been safely
closed on its important visitors. "Onto the waggons
as quickly as you can!"

At this command, both the tourists and the villagers pressed forward as one towards the waiting
empty carts – as one, that is, with the exception of
Emily Hollins.

"I don't think that I much fancy going up the
mountain road in that," objected Mrs Hollins. As
she spoke, Emily pulled a face and peered doubtfully at the horse-drawn cart which was the one
parked nearest to where the Hollinses were standing. "Pooh!" she added, wafting a hand in front of
her nose. "It *pongs*!"

"It does seem to be harbouring a rather
unpleasant odour, Emily," agreed Albert Hollins,
wrinkling his nose distastefully. "I have a feeling
that it may have been used for transporting
manure. What's your opinion, Henry?"

"It does smell as if it has had *something* that
pongs a bit inside it, Dad," admitted Henry Hollins. Then, not wanting to let a mere bad smell
delay his meeting with Count Alucard, Henry took
a firm hold of one side of the cart with both of his
hands and prepared to heave himself on board.
"But it's not *too* bad. Come on, you two!"

"I don't think I could manage to climb up into that cart, Albert – not in these shoes," murmured Emily, unhappily. "I think you're going to have to give me a leg up."

Fortunately though, as things turned out, the Hollinses did not have to make the uphill journey to the theme park's opening ceremony in that particular horse-and-cart – nor, for that matter, in any of the others either.

"All foreign tourists – follow me!" shouted Sergeant Kropotel. The police sergeant, having made his way down to the rear of the column of parked vehicles, was in the process of striding back. He twirled the pointed ends of his moustache between forefinger and thumb as he continued: "The farm vehicles are intended for the use of the Tolokovin residents only. Our highly-esteemed foreign visitors will be travelling in *style*."

"After all these long years," grunted Emil Gruff with grim satisfaction, as he snapped home the hasp on the sturdy lock which secured the gate in the high, taut, steel-mesh fence, "I've succeeded in putting the wretched beasts where they can cause me no more trouble."

The woodcutter stepped back and studied the sign which was attached to the fence:

Wolf Enclosure
KEEP OUT
These Animals Bite!

Chuckling to himself, Emil Gruff set off along the path which led towards the theme park's entrance.

"Ah-whur-whur-whurrrrr . . . !" Whimpering softly as he cowered behind a clump of bracken, Boris, the old grey wolf, watched through the fence as the woodcutter disappeared into the trees.

Several metres behind their leader, the entire pack was huddled together, gaining some small comfort from their closeness to each other but sensing also each other's trembling fear. For their entire lives, the wolves had roamed the wide expanses of the forest – knowing nothing but freedom. Suddenly, they found themselves contained behind a steel-mesh fence.

Not long before, the woodcutter and his gang of peasants, armed with their makeshift weapons, had succeeded in driving the wolf-pack up the thickly wooded ground towards the theme park. Next, they had driven the wolves between two narrowing camouflaged fences and, finally, into the recently completed steel-fenced enclosure.

The wolves had already nervously investigated the perimeter fence that now contained them. With Boris at their head, and with the adults shepherding the cubs, they had sniffed all along the steel-mesh walls that marked their prison – a wide-ranging prison, it is true, for each of the walls was over 150 metres long – but a prison, nevertheless.

Having arrived back – and recognized – the point from which they had started, the wolves had slunk into the undergrowth, dispirited, to ponder on their plight. They had watched, helpless, while Emil Gruff and his henchmen had completed the last

126

few metres of fencing. Now that Gruff and his men had gone, they looked to the wise old grey-headed Boris for salvation.

Boris, as devoid of ideas as any of his followers, sank to the ground, lowered his muzzle onto his outstretched forelegs and whimpered despairingly.

"Ah-whur-whur-whurrrrr . . .!"

"I'd hardly call *this* 'travelling in style'," whispered Emily Hollins to Albert and Henry, as the convoy, led by the sombre hearse and made up of farm-carts and waggons, set off out of the cobbled market square and along the road that wandered up the mountain.

Ernst Tigelwurst's bullock-cart was the designated tourists' transport which Police Sergeant

Alphonse Kropotel had deemed "stylish". And, despite Emily's whispered complaint, the addition of the two wooden benches did provide some small comfort.

"It might not be the last word in luxury, Emily," replied Albert Hollins. "But it's preferable to crouching on the bottom of a battered farm-cart that's been used for transporting manure across Transylvania. What do you say, Henry?"

Henry Hollins, who was so anxious to get to Castle Alucard that he would willingly have travelled there on top of a whole load of manure, gave a non-committal grunt.

"I was wondering whether a sing-song might be in order?" said Ivor Williams who was sitting next to Mr Hollins and, having overheard Emily's whisper, felt that she might need cheering up.

"What a grand idea, Ivor!" enthused Bronwyn Williams, snuggling up to her new husband and squeezing his hand. "Ivor's in the Bridgend Milkmen's Male Voice Choir," she announced proudly to the Hollinses. "He could lead us off with 'Land Of My Fathers'. He's got the best baritone voice in South Glamorgan."

"I wouldn't go quite so far as to say that, love," said Ivor Williams, with a shy smile and a modest little shrug.

"I would, Ivor!" said Bronwyn, firmly. "And I don't know why you won't admit it. I'm always saying it, and you always disagree with me. You won't get anywhere in life, Ivor, if you will insist on putting yourself down!"

"I'm not sure that a sing-song is what's needed at this moment," broke in Albert Hollins hastily, partly in order to prevent the Williamses from having their first quarrel as a married couple – and partly because he was not at all sure that their travelling companions, sitting on the other side of the bullock-cart, would be able to join in the song. "Good morning!" he added, smiling across at Hans, Frieda and Greta Grunwald.

"*Guten tag*!" replied Hans Grunwald, smiling back at Albert Hollins.

"*Buon giorno*!" said Franco Granelli, the old Italian, who was sitting next to Herr Grunwald, beaming round at everyone.

It was not long before the group of tourists were treating each other like old friends. For, while neither Emily, Albert nor Henry Hollins, nor either of the Williamses spoke any German or Italian, both the Grunwalds and the Granellis had a sufficient smattering of the English language to be able to make themselves understood.

"Perhaps a sing-song *would* be a good idea," said Emily Hollins as the convoy of carts rumbled slowly on.

"*Ja! Ja!*" said Frieda Grunwald, eagerly. "For us to sing together – this would be *sehr gut*!"

"*Si! Si!*" said Signora Granelli, briskly nodding her grey head. "Let us sing together! *Bene! Bene!*"

But as neither the Grunwalds nor the Granellis seemed to have heard of "Land Of My Fathers", an alternative had to be found.

"Do you know 'Ten Green Bottles'?" said Henry Hollins to little Greta Grunwald. "Or 'She'll Be Coming Round the Mountain When She Comes'?"

The German girl frowned, shook her head and gave a puzzled shrug.

Then, before any other suggestions could be put forward, Ernst Tigelwurst – who may have overheard and understood what was being said in the back of his cart, or may have been prompted only by the Transylvanian cloudless blue skies and the breath-taking beauty of the panoramic wooded landscape – threw back his head and burst into song himself:

> *"Sovra zora,*
> *Sovora dovra-dovrey,*
> *Sovra zokra,*
> *Sovola zokrato . . ."*

It was an old Transylvanian folk-song telling the story of a small boy and his friendship with a pack of wolves. And, while not one of the passengers in the bullock-cart had the faintest idea of the meaning of the words the carter was singing, there was a sadness in his voice that touched the hearts of all the tourists.

Then, to add to the moving occasion, all along the line of rumbling wooden vehicles, the other drivers picked up the song and joined Ernst Tigelwurst in the second verse:

> *"Sovra hobra,*
> *Sovora dovra-dushka . . ."*

As the creaking convoy of carts and waggons, led by the two proud, prancing, purple-plumed horses pulling the black, stately, silver-ornamented hearse, began the slow climb up the mountain road that meandered through the trees, the words of the old

song, coming from a score and more peasants'
throats, hung on the early-afternoon still air . . .

"*. . . Sovra zokra,*
Sovora dushka-HOY . . .!"

"Ah-whooo-OOOH . . . !" "Ah-whooo-oooh-
OOOH . . .!" "Ah-whur-whur-whurrrr . . .!"

With desperate howls and low, sad whines, the
wolves hurled themselves at the fence, shaking
the steel-mesh walls of their prison but failing to
shift the the strong, tall stanchions.

"Easy, Boris! Gently, Igor! Hush, hush – my little
ones!" Count Alucard murmured through the
tightly woven wire. It was the Count's recent arrival
that had caused the wolf-pack's frenzy.

Having spotted the enclosure through the trees,
the Count had hastened to comfort his captive
friends. But there was little that he could do there
and then to relieve their anguish. And, certainly, it
was impossible for him to set them free. The stout
lock prevented him from opening the gate and the
fence itself was far too permanent a structure for
one man to tear down with his bare hands.

"So this was the cause of all that hammering and
clattering I heard at dawn this morning," the Count
told himself. "No wonder Cousin Freddie was so
shifty . . ."

"Ah-whooo-oooh-OOOH . . . !" "Ah-whur-
whur-whurrrr . . .!" "Ah-whooo-OOOH . . .!"

"Easy! Easy! Have patience, my poor children of
the night! Believe me, my dear ones, I will see to it
that you are released from this monstrous place and
without delay!"

131

With which, Count Alucard turned and sped off through the trees, as fast as his spindly legs would carry him and with his long, black cloak flapping out behind, towards the castle.

10

"I say, Higgins, old fruit, this is really spiffing, don't you know!" exclaimed Lord Frederick Allardyce Alucard – at the same time unable to prevent himself from giving a little involuntary shiver as he peered around at his surroundings.

"Indeed it is, milord," murmured the butler, with a gulp. "But if I may be allowed to say so – also a trifle spooky!"

The hour had almost come for the grand opening ceremony at Vampire Park and Lord Freddie was making a last minute-inspection of the theme park's main attractions. With the ever-present Higgins hovering just behind his shoulder, his lordship had dared to venture, for the very first time, down the worn, stone steps and into the damp, dank subterranean chamber where the past masters of Alucard Castle lay in their coffins.

In readiness for the expected flood of tourists, the underground chamber was lit by many candles, flickering in age-old iron sconces and in ghostly fashion, on the grey-stone walls of the gloomy vaulted chamber. They illuminated the remains of all the dead Count Alucards from times long past. These blood-drinking evil vampires now lay for all

to see in their crimson-lined coffins – each skeleton with a sharp-pointed wooden stake embedded in its rib-cage.

A vampire can only be killed – or so legend has it – by having a wooden stake driven into its heart while the monster is asleep. If the stake were ever to be removed, then again according to legend, mouldering flesh would cover the bones and the vampire would return to life . . .

Lord Freddie did not believe in such silly superstitions. All the same, he was not tempted to test the legend by reaching into a coffin and plucking a stake from its resting-place. "Not that anything could possibly happen to me if I were to do so," he assured himself. "All the same, it is better to be safe than sorry . . ."

Then, just as he was pondering over the awful possibility of what *might* possibly occur if there *did* happen to be any substance to the legend, his thoughts were suddenly interrupted by the sound of huge beating wings. Glancing up, he glimpsed with horror a large, black-winged figure silhouetted in the daylight that filtered in at the top of the steps.

"Ah-whooo-oooh-OOOH . . .!" moaned the apparition that barred the exit, flapping its dark membraneous wings again and causing the candles to flicker all the more.

"Wh-wh-what is it, Higgins?" stuttered Lord Freddie, grabbing at Higgins' sleeve and thrusting the butler between himself and the figure that loomed above them.

"*Ah-whooo-OOOH-oooh . . .!*" Slowly, the dark shape began to advance down towards the master and manservant at the foot of the worn stone steps.

"Have no fear, milord," announced the butler, as the figure came far enough into the tomb for its features to be visible in the candlelight below. "It is merely Mr Brannigan."

"B-B-B-Brannigan?" mumbled Lord Freddie, still cowering behind Higgins' back. "Are you absolutely *sure*?"

"It is indeed Mr Brannigan, milord," replied Higgins. "In his vampire disguise and playing a prank upon us both, I sadly fear."

"Don't ever – *ever* – attempt another trick like that, Brannigan!" snapped Lord Freddie, venturing out at last from behind the butler's back.

"Sorry, your lordship," said the stuntman, trying hard to suppress a snigger as he folded the two ungainly plastic wings, strapped to his arms, in front of his black-garbed body. "It seemed like a good opportunity to try out my Count Alucard costume." Butch Brannigan strutted proudly, body-builder fashion, in front of Lord Freddie, and added: "What do you think?"

In addition to the plastic wings, the stuntman was wearing clothes identical to those worn by the real Count Alucard: black formal suit, black patent leather shoes, white frilly shirt and a white bow tie. He was also wearing white make-up on his face and his lips and eyes had been reddened. Two plastic fangs protruded over his lower lip.

"I suppose it will suffice," admitted Lord Freddie, grudgingly, having re-affixed his monocle which had dropped out several moments before as his eyes had widened in horror. "Was there anything else?"

"I'm going to try a practice-flight down the high-wire before the theme park opens," said the stuntman. "I wondered if you'd like to watch me?"

"If I must," replied the master of Castle Alucard, glancing at his gold wristwatch. "But you'd better get a move on – our invited guests *and* the paying public will be arriving shortly." Lord Freddie brushed past Butch Brannigan and then, when he was halfway up the stone steps, turned and looked down again. "But I'm giving you a solemn warning, Brannigan – one more jape like the one you tried in here, and you'll find a sizeable stoppage in your wage packet when pay day comes around. Is that understood?"

"Fully understood, your lordship – and comprehensively taken on board," replied the stuntman smarmily, raising a forefinger to his forehead.

"Good!" Lord Freddie paused. From where he stood, looking past Butch Brannigan and Higgins, he could see the inside of all the crimson-lined black coffins on either side of the shadowy chamber. The skulls of the skeletons of the Alucards past appeared to wink at him as the candlelight cast flickering shadows in their empty eye-sockets. Lord Freddie experienced the same sort of shiver all along his spine as the the one that he had felt when he had first entered the tomb. "It *is* spooky down here," he murmured to himself. "I don't know what sort of effect it's going to have on the paying public – but it sure enough gives me goose pimples!"

With which, and followed by his manservant and Butch Brannigan, Lord Frederick Allardyce Alucard scuttled up the few remaining steps that led out of the dank, dark, cheerless burial chamber and, thankfully, into sunlight, blue skies and open air.

"Wheee-eeeh-EEEEH . . .!" Head-first, on outstretched plastic wings, Butch Brannigan let out a scream of sheer exhilaration as he jumped off the castle's topmost turreted roof and careered, by means of the pulley attached to his harness, down the taut steel rope that stretched to the ground. Skimming over the tops of the smaller rides, the sideshows and the fast-food restaurants, he could see the upturned faces of the theme-park's operators gazing at him, open-mouthed.

He came to earth, rather clumsily at this first attempt, and staggered for several strides before

finally coming to a halt behind the entrance to the vampire rollercoaster. Unstrapping himself from his harness, the stuntman strode jauntily across to where Lord Freddie, with the ever attentive Higgins in attendance, waited in the shadow of the rollercoaster's towering framework.

"Not bad, eh?" said Butch Brannigan, oozing false modesty and striking his usual show-off bodybuilder's pose.

But before Lord Freddie could comment upon Butch Brannigan's performance as the daylight flying vampire, an angry voice called out across the theme park.

"*Freddie*!" It was Count Alucard himself, striding towards the trio on his lanky legs. "I've been looking for you everywhere – I want a word with you!"

"What is it now, old chap?" replied the master of Castle Alucard, blinking through his monocle in feigned surprise. "If it's about the non-arrival at the gift shop of those black baseball caps with the gold-embroidered vampire motifs, the manufacturer has apologized and promised us most faithfully . . ."

"It has got nothing to do with baseball caps – and well you know it!" snapped the Count. "I want to know what on earth you imagine you are up to – having that disgusting cage constructed and then putting all the wolves inside it?"

"My dear good fellow," began Lord Freddie, slipping an arm around his cousin's shoulders and attempting to lead him away from, and out of ear-shot of, Butch Brannigan and Higgins. " 'Cage' is rather a harsh word, isn't it? I consider it to be more of a park. And, surely, you don't imagine for a single second that we can run a successful theme park surrounded by a forest overrun with danger-ous wild animals?"

"Those wolves have never so much as bared their teeth at a single human being, Freddie," replied Count Alucard curtly, shrugging off his cousin's attempted conciliatory arm and adding: "Unless, of course, that person has attempted to harm them first."

"All right! All right! Point taken, old bean," mur-mured Lord Freddie. "My goodness me! I don't know what all the fuss is about. They'll be well-fed and well-looked after in that enclosure. They'll be far better off, in fact, than having to fend for them-selves – and they'll be an added attraction for the visitors to Vampire Park."

"The wolf-pack belongs in the wild, Freddie,"

said Count Alucard firmly. His voice rose as he continued: "I want the key that opens the gate to that enclosure."

"Calm down, cousin!" muttered Lord Freddie, glancing around uneasily. "People are listening."

In addition to Butch Brannigan and Higgins, several Tolokovinite villagers, employed as theme park operators and dressed in the official uniform of peasant smock and trousers, calf-length boots, "Vampire Park" armbands and similarly emblazoned shiny-peaked caps, were also showing an interest in the argument developing between the past master of Castle Alucard and his successor.

"I don't care who hears me, Freddie," replied Count Alucard stubbornly, holding out a hand palm upwards, pale slim fingers extended. "I want that key. I want it *now*. And I won't take 'No' for an answer!"

There was total silence for several seconds as the two men: the tall, thin, dark-haired, solemn-faced Count Alucard and his shorter, stouter, curly-haired, monocled English cousin stood their ground and stared hard into each other's eyes. Then, gradually, the silence was broken by the sound of several hundred voices raised in song and coming out of the trees beyond the theme park's entrance.

"Sovra hobra,
Sovora dovra-dushka . . ."

The convoy of carts and waggons bringing the first day's visitors to Vampire Park had made its way up the winding mountain road and was lumbering through the forest towards the theme park's entrance. The local peasants, packed inside the vehicles, had added their voices to the drivers' song:

> *"Zovra zokra,*
> *Sovola zokrato . . .!"*

"Look here, old sport, we shouldn't be quarrelling, you know," Lord Freddie's voice took on a wheedling tone as he attempted another tack. "After all – we are *cousins*. We're the last two Alucards left alive, old chap. We're *family*. Good heavens above – if I'd known that you cared so much about those mangy miserable wolves, I would never have had that enclosure built. As soon as this afternoon is over, I'll do exactly as you ask and set them free – how does that suit you?"

"Why not do it now?" replied Count Alucard, puzzled by his cousin's sudden change of attitude and only half-convinced that he was telling him the truth.

"Because I haven't got the key about my person, old bean. And because we've got visitors arriving at any second." Lord Freddie paused and nodded over at Butch Brannigan, dressed like Count Alucard but with the addition of the plastic wings. "You wouldn't want to spoil our tourists' day by letting them see *two* vampire counts strolling around the theme park, would you?"

"Not really," mumbled the Count.

"Well then – why don't you take yourself off behind the gift shop counter, slip into a T-shirt, and help to make everyone's day a success by lying low for the afternoon?"

"Very well, Freddie – if you'll give me your solemn oath that you'll release the wolves as soon as the afternoon is over?"

"I've already *said* so, haven't I? I'm an Alucard, aren't I? And isn't an Alucard's word as good as his bond?" It was an incontestable statement. "*Really*, cousin! It hurts me to imagine that you could doubt my intentions for a single second!"

"I'm awfully sorry, Freddie," said Count Alucard, instantly ashamed of himself for having questioned his cousin's integrity. "I'll do exactly as you say. I'll be behind the gift shop counter, if you should need me."

"That's the spirit, old sport," Lord Freddie murmured with an approving smile then, as the Count strode off towards the gift shop, he turned towards the stuntman. "Brannigan!"

"Yes, your lordship?"

"Take yourself back up on the roof and get ready for your very first public performance."

"I can hardly wait, your lordship!" The stuntman strutted off towards the castle.

"And Brannigan . . .?"

"Your lordship?"

"Come here!" Lord Freddie beckoned the stuntman back towards him and lowered his voice, the smile fading from his face, replaced by a scowl. "As soon as this afternoon's shenanigans are over, there's another little task I'd like you to perform."

"If it's something that needs a bit of muscle power," replied Butch Brannigan dropping on one knee and raising a bulky forearm in front of his face, "I'm your man."

"Count Alucard is getting just a shade too big for his shiny patent leather footwear," said Lord Freddie, his right eye glinting fiercely behind his gold-rimmed monocle. "I'd like you to put a stop to his continual confounded complaining."

"No sooner said than taken care of, your lordship," replied the stuntman bounding up onto his feet and brandishing an enormous clenched fist. "I'll give him a taste of this."

"If I may be allowed to venture an opinion, milord," murmured Higgins, drawing closer to his employer as Butch Brannigan set out again towards the castle, "a proposition of which I am entirely in approval."

"Thank you, Higgins." Lord Freddie let out an unpleasant little snigger. "And now – I fancy I hear the waggons at our portals. If you'll be so good as to trot across and inform those chappies at the entrance they can open the gates, we can start the turnstiles ticking over and start earning ourselves some well-deserved cash!"

"Ah-aaah-AAAAAH . . ." The concerted gasp of admiring approval rose from the crowd as they peered up at the large vampire cruising over their heads on wide black outstretched wings.

Butch Brannigan's trip down the overhead wire was intended as a prelude to the official opening ceremony. The paying public, local peasants and foreign tourists alike, were gathered behind a rope which served to keep them at a distance from the important guests seated on the temporary platform.

From the volume of applause which followed quickly after the admiring gasp, it appeared that all of the onlookers had been delighted with the stuntman's performance.

All of the onlookers that is – except for one.

"It isn't a *real* vampire," whispered Henry Hollins to his parents. Henry, Albert and Emily had succeeded in securing a good vantage point in the front row and next to the rope. "*Real* vampires don't come out until it's dark – I thought *everyone* knew that," sniffed Henry.

"Hush, Henry," hissed Emily at her son. "Real vampire or not, I thought it was very entertaining – considering that we didn't have to pay extra for it."

"Not bad at all," agreed Albert Hollins. "Mind you – when you consider how much they charged us to get inside the gates, I don't suppose they had the cheek to make us pay to watch a chap slide down a wire."

"Oh dear me!" said Emily, raising her eyebrows. "Was it *very* expensive?"

"Enough to make a sizeable hole in the grobeks in my pocket," said Albert Hollins ruefully.

At that moment, having touched down out of sight behind the Vampire Ride's pay box, Butch Brannigan reappeared, minus his harness. He strutted proudly across towards the VIP platform.

"You will all be pleased to hear that our resident vampire will also be available to autograph your souvenir brochures," announced Lord Freddie, rising to his feet at the stuntman's approach. "He will also be happy to answer any questions you might care to ask him. Can I ask you all to give another big hand for his recent death-defying flight! Ladies and gentlemen – Count Alucard!"

"*Bravo*! *Bravo*!" shouted Signor and Signora Granelli.

"*Wunderbar*!" cried the Grunwalds.

"Great stuff isn't it, look you!" yelled Ivor and Bronwyn Williams.

"Well done that vampire!" bellowed Albert and Emily Hollins forgetting, for the moment, how much their entry into the park had cost them.

"*Prushka*! *Prushka*!" roared the local peasants.

Up on the platform, Butch Brannigan posed and postured, revelling in the renewed applause. Everyone, it seemed, was appreciative of the stuntman's slide down the high wire. Everyone, that is – with one exception.

"That's not Count Alucard!" exclaimed Henry Hollins indignantly. "He's an impostor."

"Hush, Henry," said Emily. "I'm sure that the gentleman in the monocle knows what he's talking about – he would hardly say it was Count Alucard if it wasn't."

"But it *isn't* the Count, Mum!" insisted Henry. "You *know* it isn't! You've met the real Count Alucard. You too, Dad – more than once!"

"Perhaps this chap's the other chap's brother," said Albert Hollins with a shrug.

"Count Alucard hasn't *got* a brother, Dad! He'd have told me if he had."

So far, the applause for the stuntman's efforts had drowned out Henry's voice, but as the sound of the cheers and clapping died away, his protestations were beginning to be heard. Several people were casting curious glances in the Hollins' direction.

"Hush, Henry!" hissed Albert, brusquely. "I'm sure your mother's right – they wouldn't say this chap was someone that he wasn't. They wouldn't fob us off with an impostor . . ." Mr Hollins paused, then repeated: " . . . Not at the price they charged us to come in here in the first place."

Up on the platform, Lord Freddie was holding up his hands for total silence.

"Now do be quiet, Henry!" hissed Albert Hollins, fiercely. "I'd like to hear what's being said."

"Visitors to Vampire Park – I bid you welcome!" began Lord Freddie. "But before I declare this theme park well and truly open, I know that Mayor Rumboll has a few words that he would like to say to you." Henri Rumboll, sitting on Lord Freddie's right, shuffled his bottom, importantly, on the seat of his chair while his lordship glanced down at the important person sitting on his left, and then continued: "And Sergeant Kropotel has also got a few words that he deems appropriate for the occasion." Lord Freddie paused again while Alphonse Kropotel twirled the ends of his moustache. At the same time, Eric Horowitz, who was also sitting on the platform, feeling himself ignored, cleared his throat as a sign that he too had composed a sentence or two he would like to add. "But before Mayor Rumboll, or Sergeant Kropotel – or anyone else for that matter – says anything at all, there are just a couple of things that I would like to say myself . . ."

"This is *boring*, Dad," whispered Henry Hollins. "I'll see you later. I'm going for a walk."

"Don't stray too far, Henry," said Emily anxiously. "And don't be gone for more than a couple of minutes – I'm sure these speeches won't take very long."

But Henry Hollins, knowing that speeches had a habit of going on interminably, had already wriggled through the crowds and was setting off to explore the empty theme park by himself.

11

Count Alucard gazed gloomily into the mirror in the back of the gift shop and was grateful, for once, that he could not see his own image gazing, gloomily, back at him.

Vampires, as everyone knows, do not possess a mirror-image. In fact, should you ever have cause to harbour any doubts, one certain way of knowing if you are in the company of a vampire, is to hold up a mirror in front of that person's face. If he, or she, has not got a mirror-image, then the best thing that you can do is run! Unless, of course, that person should chance to be Count Alucard – in which circumstance you would be perfectly safe.

The reason that the Count was grateful, on that particular afternoon, that he could not see his reflected image in the gift shop mirror was because he had no wish to see himself in the ridiculous T-shirt he was having to wear:

I'VE BEEN TO
VAMPIRE PARK
AND ALL
THAT I CAME BACK WITH
WERE A BITE
AND THIS LOUSY T-SHIRT!

On the t-shirt: I'VE BEEN TO VAMPIRE PARK AND ALL I CAME BACK WITH WERE A BIT

"How distasteful!" sighed the Count.

It really was too bad of Lord Freddie to condemn the Count to spend all of his time in the gift shop, with its ghastly little bottles of imitation blood, and its vampire whoopee cushions, and its singularly unattractive plastic joke fangs ...

But there were more important matters in hand, the Count told himself. First and foremost, there was the question of his friends, the wolves. Provided that Lord Freddie kept his word and released the pack from its captivity that very afternoon, then Count Alucard was prepared to forgive his English cousin for quite a number of things. And what reason was there to doubt what his cousin said? As Freddie himself had pointed out, he was an Alucard – and an Alucard's word *was* as good as his bond . . . All the same, his cousin's manner and actions over the last few weeks had begun to raise suspicions in Count Alucard's mind . . .

The Count's ponderings were interrupted by the sound of movement outside the gift shop. How odd? Surely the opening ceremony could not be over already? Count Alucard knew that there were speeches to be made, not only by Lord Freddie but also by Henri Rumboll and Sergeant Kropotel. The Count knew enough about Tolokovin ways to realize that if both the mayor and the police sergeant were intending to speak, then it would be difficult to prevent Eric Horowitz from adding several pompous words as well . . .

No, the theme park's opening ceremony would not be over for some time yet. So who could be hovering outside the gift shop door? Count Alucard lifted the counter-flap, quietly, and set out to investigate.

"Henry Hollins!" gasped the Count, amazed at finding his young friend – whom he had imagined to be home at 42, Nicholas Nickleby Close, Staplewood – standing by the revolving souvenir stand outside the gift shop.

"Count Alucard!" gulped Henry Hollins, at least half a second later – for it took that amount of time for him to recognize his noble friend in the unlikely T-shirt.

"But what on earth are you doing here?" stammered the Count.

"I was reading this," said Henry Hollins, holding up the Vampire Park souvenir booklet he had taken down from the stand. "I was just coming in to pay for it."

"No, no, no, my dear young friend. I meant, what brings you to Transylvania – and, more to the point, out of all the theme park gift shops in the world, what quirk of circumstance has brought you to my doorstep?"

"I didn't know that you were here, Count," said Henry. "But now that you come to mention it, *why* are you working in the gift shop? And what are you doing wearing that silly T-shirt instead of your proper clothes? And who's that man with the stupid plastic wings? And why is he pretending to be you?"

"Ah! So many questions!" Count Alucard raised his hands and his pale, slim fingers fluttered in the air expressively as he let out a long, sad sigh. "Thereby hangs a tale – and rather a long one too, I fear . . ."

"That's all right – there's plenty of time for you to tell me all about it, Count," said Henry Hollins, leading the way into the gift shop. "That opening ceremony looks as if it could drag on all afternoon."

"And finally, and in conclusion . . ." droned Henri Rumboll gazing up at the sky and about to launch into yet another boring anecdote.

"That's the third time he's said 'Finally, and in conclusion'," whispered Emily to Albert Hollins.

"I know," groaned Mr Hollins then, nodding across at Sergeant Kropotel, he continued: "And that chap in the funny uniform hasn't said his piece yet. *And* it wouldn't surprise me in the least, Emily, if there were others on that platform wanting to put in their two-pennyworth. If you want my opinion,

151

our Henry made the right decision when he made a run for it."

"Speaking of Henry," murmured Emily, casting an anxious glance over her shoulder. "I wonder where he's got to?"

"Oh, you know Henry," said Mr Hollins philosophically. "He'll turn up when it suits him. One thing's for certain – he'll keep well away from here while this ceremony's dragging on *ad infinitum* . . ."

"And finally, and in conclusion . . ." droned Henri Rumboll yet again.

As the mayor of Tolokovin paused for breath, a loud, concerted sigh of boredom rose from the captive audience contained inside the roped enclosure.

"And that, my dear young friend, is all there is to tell." Count Alucard's thin shoulders drooped beneath his T-shirt as if bowed down with all the worries in the world. Leaning despondently on the gift shop counter, he had related to Henry Hollins all of the events that had resulted in his present sad and sorry situation. Beginning with the history, which Lord Freddie had recounted, of their English ancestor's life in Whitby and in Bradford, then going on to explain all that had happened since the English lord had arrived at Alucard Castle, with Higgins, his old retainer, to claim all that belonged to him – and ending with the news of how the wolves had been driven inside the steel-mesh fenced enclosure. "And the awful truth of the matter is, Henry, that my English cousin has a perfect right to do all this – Lord Frederick Allardyce Alucard is the rightful heir to all of these estates."

"I don't think that he has, Count," said Henry Hollins, with a puzzled frown. "And I don't believe that he is the rightful heir to anything – not here in Transylvania."

"Whatever do you mean?"

"Haven't you read this?" asked Henry Hollins, holding up the booklet he had brought in with him from the revolving stand outside the gift shop.

"No. Those items only arrived this morning, along with some baseball caps we've been waiting for. I only opened the packing case about half an hour ago. And I popped a couple of those booklets outside with the souvenir postcards without even giving them a second glance." The Count extended a slim hand. "May I see it, please?"

"Of course you can."

Henry passed the booklet across to the Count who studied the title on the cover:

A CONCISE HISTORY OF THE ALUCARDS
(And other Vampires)
by
Professor Otto Von Bronstein

"I have heard of the professor," said Count Alucard. "He is the world's leading authority on vampirical matters. What does the booklet say, Henry?"

"I'll tell you first what it *doesn't* say," said Henry firmly. "It doesn't say anything at all about there being an English branch of the Alucards. According to Professor Bronstein, your ancestor who went to Whitby only stayed in England for a few weeks – he didn't marry anyone and he certainly didn't have an English son. It's all on page two – read it for yourself."

"But if this booklet is correct, Henry – and why should we doubt the word of such a learned man," said the Count as his sharp, black eyes scanned the appropriate page, "then Lord Freddie is not who he purports to be."

"It wouldn't surprise me in the least, Count, if Lord Frederick Allardyce Alucard should turn out to be as big an impostor as that man with the silly plastic wings."

"And the fellow that calls himself the butler could also be a fake!" murmured the Count excitedly. "If only we could prove it, my young friend, we could send the villains packing!"

"Perhaps there is a way that we could do that too, Count," said Henry Hollins, taking the booklet out of Count Alucard's slim fingers. After flicking through a couple more pages, he located an important paragraph. "Look at this," he continued. "It says that your ancestor who went to Whitby is buried here, in the Alucard family tomb."

"Then there is only one way of finding out if that is true," said the Count, tugging off the T-shirt and reaching for his white bow tie which he had placed, for safe-keeping, underneath the counter and on top of a box labelled: "Joke Plastic Vampire Fangs – Various Sizes". "And that is by going down there," Count Alucard continued, "and seeing for oneself."

"Can I come with you?" asked Henry Hollins eagerly.

"I fear not, Henry," said Count Alucard, gravely shaking his head. "I would not wish Lord Freddie –

as he calls himself – to observe me crossing the theme park, and so I'll make my way down into the vaults by a route that few people are aware exists. But it could prove dangerous."

"If it's dangerous, Count Alucard," said Henry Hollins bravely, "then you might need my help."

"Thank you for that kind offer, my dear, good, kind friend," replied the Count, patting Henry on the shoulder. At the same time, and unseen by Henry, Count Alucard brushed away a tear. Being a vampire, and therefore loathed and feared by most members of the human race, the Count was quite touched at Henry's ready willingness to face danger with him and on his behalf. "I had always believed that I could count upon your services in adversity," the Count continued, "but on this occasion, you can serve me best by remaining here and looking after the gift shop. It might be considered suspicious by our enemies, were it to be left unattended."

"If that is what you want, Count," said Henry Hollins, trying hard not to show his disappointment.

"It is exactly what I want," replied the Count, taking down his scarlet-lined black cloak from behind the gift-shop door and slipping it around his thin shoulders. Count Alucard's dark eyes sparkled and, for the moment, he was his old self again. "Be on your guard, Henry Hollins!" he exclaimed, striking a theatrical pose as he paused by the gift-shop door, then added: "The game's afoot!"

As the door creaked softly shut behind his friend, Henry Hollins gave a little gulp. He would have much preferred to have accompanied the Count on

155

the adventure – whatever it was. In truth, Henry felt less brave now that he was alone in the spookily green-lit gift shop with its strange collection of souvenir goods: eyeless bat-masks gazed down at him from the walls, while rubbery, black vampire bats swung gently, in a draught, on their elastic from the ceiling.

However, Henry Hollins had given the Count his word. He had agreed to look after the shop in his friend's absence, and that was exactly what he intended to do. Disregarding the plastic bats swinging spookily above his head, Henry took off the gaily-coloured holiday sweatshirt he was wearing, tugged on the shop-assistant's uniform T-shirt, and took up his position behind the counter.

"Ah-whoo-OOO-ooooh . . .!"

"What was that?" queried Karl Gustaffe, the Assistant Wolf-Keeper at Vampire Park, fearfully.

"Only a wolf, you fool!" growled Emil Gruff, Wolf-Keeper in Chief.

"I didn't mean the wolf howl," replied Gustaffe. "I meant the noise that came before it."

"What kind of a noise?"

"A sort of snapping sound – as if somebody had stepped on a twig."

"I didn't hear anything – it must have been your imagination," snapped the woodcutter turned Wolf-Keeper in Chief. Gruff was anxious to get back to his cottage, deep in the forest, where he had left an iron pot full of goat's-meat and turnip stew simmering on his pot-bellied stove. "I have to go," he added. "I have important business to attend to."

Left by himself outside the fenced enclosure, Karl Gustaffe felt his keeper's stick tremble in his hand as he watched his boss stride off along the forest path. Gustaffe did not like Gruff, but he would rather have had his company than be left on his own.

Karl Gustaffe had not begun that day as an Assistant Wolf-Keeper. By rights, Gustaffe was a master-baker. He much preferred the heat and light and closeness of his Tolokovin bakehouse to the cool, shadowy depths of the far-reaching forest, where the silence was punctuated by wolf howls and the curious inexplicable sounds of snapping twigs.

Karl Gustaffe had been recruited from the bake-house by Gruff at dawn that morning. First, to drive the wolves into the enclosure and then, to his dismay, to remain behind when the others had gone, to act as Assistant Wolf-Keeper. Karl Gustaffe had not wanted to be an Assistant Wolf-Keeper, but he did not dare to argue with Emil Gruff.

"Ah-whoo-OOO-ooooh . . .!"

"What was that?" muttered Gustaffe again, and to himself, as this time the sound of a snapping twig came after the wolf howl and not before it. The Assistant Wolf-Keeper peered nervously into the pine trees, first one way – then off in the opposite direction. Had the baker turned Wolf-Keeper thought to glance above his head, he would have seen the cause of the snapping twigs.

Gripping tightly with his hands and knees, Count Alucard was edging his way, centimetre by centimetre, along the lowest bough of a towering pine tree which overhung the steel-mesh fence. He had scrambled up the tree trunk some minutes before, while both Emil Gruff and Karl Gustaffe had been looking in another direction. Now, having crossed over the fence, as the bough began to sag beneath his weight, the Count lowered first his feet, then his body and, finally, released his hold. He dropped onto the soft bed of pine needles below inside the enclosure, almost – but not quite – without a sound.

"What was that?" quavered Karl Gustaffe for a third time, on the other side of the fence.

"Ah-whoo-oooh-OOOOH . . .!"

This time, the howl was followed, not long after, by the sound of thudding paws and bodies crashing through bracken. Then, as the entire wolf-pack hurtled through the undergrowth and seemingly in his direction, regardless of the fact that a stout steel fence stood between himself and them, Karl Gustaffe took to his heels and fled – and he would not stop running, he promised himself, until he was safely inside his friendly bakehouse with its green door shut and bolted behind him.

Inside the wolf enclosure, the pack broke from cover and sped excitedly towards Count Alucard. Led, as always, by the wily old Boris, and with Droshka, Ilya, Lubchik, Ivan, Igor, Olga, Relka, Mikhail – and all the others – close behind. The yapping cubs brought up the rear.

Looking to the Count to release them from their plight, the wolves formed a tight-packed mass around his legs, struggling against each other as they attempted to leap up and lick his face – and would have bowled him clean off his feet, had he

not been kept upright by their own sheer weight surrounding him.

"Easy, *easy*, Relka! Gently, Igor! Down, Dushka! Patience, Lubchik! Steadily, *steadily*, my darlings!" Count Alucard put out a soothing hand and, speaking softly, calmed each of the animals in turn until, at last, they stood still, silent and in an attentive circle around him.

"This way, my children."

With the wolf-pack padding in his wake, Count Alucard strode off up the enclosure and in the direction of the theme park. When they had progressed some hundred metres, or thereabouts, the Count came to a stop at a spot where the trees thinned out and the ground rose steeply. Raising his eyes, the Count could see over the ridge to where, not far ahead, the steel-mesh fence ran parallel with the wooden palisade which surrounded Vampire Park.

Watched by the wolves, Count Alucard selected a stout stick from several which were lying on the ground. The one he chose was about as thick as, and slightly longer than, a walking-cane. Then, moving slowly along the foot of the rise, he began to jab the stick into the earth at about his own chest height. For several metres, the stick sank easily into the earth and then, after some dozen or so attempts, he struck something hard. Another couple of exploratory jabs, both striking the same solid object underneath, convinced the Count that he had found what he was seeking.

"Here, my children!" he cried, using his hands to tear at the wall of earth and show the wolves what he required of them. "Dig, my children of the night! Dig!"

Boris, as always, was first to take up the task. Planting his rear legs firmly on the ground, he began to burrow, fast and furiously, into the ridge. One by one, the stronger members of the pack joined in until there was a solid mass of fur and claw and muscle, shifting the earth in front and kicking it to the rear.

Gradually, the stout oak door which had been concealed behind the wall of earth came into view. And behind the door was a long, dark stone-walled passage which had lain unused for centuries . . .

12

Ever since his childhood, Count Alucard had known of the existence of the secret passage that led from his family tomb into the forest. Indeed, he was aware of several hidden tunnels which had their beginnings in his forebears' final resting place. Being an underground chamber, the Alucard vault was an ideal location as the meeting point for the honeycomb of secret passages. There was a tunnel which led from the vault to underneath the castle's coach house – he had had cause to make use of that particular path some several months before. Another passageway ran from the vault, undeneath the courtyard and then twisted and turned, through the thick castle walls, into the library.

The existence of these hidden entrances and exits had been revealed to the Count by his late father, in exactly the same way that the knowledge of them had been handed down by Alucards throughout history. They had been devised originally by Count Draculas long centuries before – most of them built when the castle itself had been constructed. They had been intended as escape routes by the early vampire Counts when the angry, vengeance-seeking peasants had come a-calling up the mountain-side.

Count Alucard could understand why the peasants, in days gone by, had been consumed by an angry urge that sought to destroy his blood-drinking ancestors – but it saddened him that on several occasions, and despite the fact that he was a harmless vegetarian, the present-day superstitious villagers had swarmed up the mountain-side intent on destroying both Castle Alucard and himself . . .

"Commit all of these passages to memory, my boy," the late Count Alucard had counselled his young son. "Guard their secret well – one day, they may serve to save your life."

It had not occurred to Count Alucard's father that, one day, one of the passages might help the entire Tolokovin forest wolf-pack escape from imprisonment.

It was now Count Alucard's intention to put the secret tunnel to that very use.

By the time the burrowing wolves had scooped sufficient earth behind them to clear completely the hidden door in the mountain ridge, the afternoon was drifting towards early evening.

As Count Alucard peered along the tunnel,

which lay beyond the door, the sun was dipping down towards the mountain top. The daylight filtering along the passage was already fading. There was no time to be lost. Beckoning the wolves to follow him, the Count set off at once along the narrow passage which, with the absence of any light source up ahead, grew gloomier at every twist and turn. Before he had gone very far, the darkness closed in completely and he was forced to slow his pace and feel his way along the cold, stone tunnel wall.

He was also hampered by the wolves' reluctance to venture further along the passage. Living their lives in the open air, their natural instinct was to back away from the close-walled darkness. The Count was forced to pause with every few steps that he took and urge the pack, with soft cajoling murmurs, to follow where he led.

Although he judged that it could not have been more than a hundred metres, at the very most, from the tunnel's entrance to the vault, it seemed to be taking him an interminable time to complete that distance.

At last, to his immense relief, the Count's exploratory, fluttering fingers made contact with a solid wall which barred his path. He knew that he had reached the end of the tunnel – but where, he wondered, was the door, or aperture, that would take him beyond the wall and into the vault on the other side?

"Ah-whur-whur-whuuur . . .!"

"Hush! Hush, my children!" the Count murmured to the wolves who were now whimpering softly as they crowded close behind him. "I will have you out of here in two shakes of a cub's tail, that is a solemn promise . . . Ahhh!"

Count Alucard let out a sigh of relief as, in the blackness, his hands touched a metal ring. He grasped the ring tightly and tugged hard. From somewhere inside the wall, there came the muffled sound of a rusting chain grinding over rusting cogs – and then, thankfully, a glimmer of light appeared in the tunnel. Moving on some ancient mechanism, a small section of the wall, at about the Count's waist-height, had shifted leaving a space just big enough for a man to get his head and shoulders through.

"Ah-whur-whur-whuuuUUUR . . .!"

The wolves' whimperings increased in volume and anxiety as they too glimpsed the light. They guessed that it marked their path to freedom. Count Alucard could feel the weight of the entire pack pushing restlessly at the back of his legs.

"Patience! Have patience, my dears!" Count Alucard whispered sharply over his shoulder.

Although the flickering light came from his family vault and not far from the entrance to the vault lay the edge of the open forest, and freedom, Count Alucard knew that he still needed to proceed with caution. He would have to assure himself that the coast was clear before he dare venture into the tomb.

Stooping down, holding his breath and crossing his slim fingers, the Count thrust his head through the space in the wall. Thankfully, for the moment at least, the tomb stood empty. But judging by the sound of the theme park's fairground music that was drifting into the vault through the open door at the top of the steps, Count Alucard knew that it would not be empty for long. He guessed that the opening ceremony had ended and that Vampire Park was now open for business.

Count Alucard had guessed correctly.

The boring speeches having dragged on for most of the afternoon, the opening ceremony had ended only a few minutes before. The theme park's visitors, having been penned for hours inside the rope enclosure, now felt the need to stretch their legs and, also, to savour the last few rays of the setting sun. They had no desire, at that immediate moment, to investigate the gloomy final resting place of Alucards long dead. They preferred to wander round the rides and sidestalls. Some of them, having worked up appetites, were keen to sample what the park's fast-food outlets had to offer: the goose-burgers, the shrubel-cakes, the raspberry flavoured goat's-milkshakes.

But that was a situation that would not last for long. The first inquisitive sightseers would soon clatter down the worn stone steps to shiver with excitement at the ghoulish delights on offer in the Alucard family vault.

Realizing that every second was important, Count Alucard glanced down and saw that the entrance hole was situated in a shadowy part of the candlelit tomb and about three metres from the ground. From this height, Count Alucard could see all of his forebears' skeletons resident in their coffins, each with a sharp-pointed wooden stake transfixed between its ribs.

"You poor, poor fellows," sighed Count Alucard. Then, mindful of the awful deeds that each one of his ancestors had been guilty of, he added: "But I fear you all deserved the fate that sadly befell each one of you . . ."

Turning round, the Count slid both of his long legs, and then his body, through the hole. Taking care not to disturb either the coffin, or its gruesome inhabitant resting there, he lowered his neatly-shod feet towards the shelf below which, he surmised, had been intentionally positioned as a stepping-stone between the secret entrance and the ancient mosaic floor.

Once on the shelf, it was Count Alucard's intention to raise his arms and assist the wolves, one by one, through the hole and down onto the floor. Once he had got the pack safely down, he would lead them up the stone steps, then back into the forest and release them into the wild.

But what the Count intended and what actually happened were two entirely different things. As soon as the Count's head was clear of the hole, the wolves were given their first unhindered glimpse of the vault beyond the wall. They were all instantly and eagerly excited. Ilya and Lubchik, headstrong as always, leaped simultaneously over Boris and tried to squeeze through the hole at one and the same time. But the hole was not big enough for them both and so the two young wolves found themselves wedged. Not only were they both dismayed at being momentarily held fast, but their bodies had again shut out the light from the rest of the pack behind them.

"Ah-whoo-oooh-**OOOOOH** . . .!"

The wolf-pack, once more in total darkness, let out a concerted howl as it again thrust forward, pressing hard against the rear-ends of the two wolves jammed in the escape hole.

"Easy! Take it steadily, my children!" Count Alucard called urgently, fearful of what was about to happen – and entirely unable to prevent it.

Propelled by the weight of the others pressing behind them, Ilya and Lubchik shot out of the secret entrance like two corks popping from a single bottle into the vault below. Ilya sprawled, four legs wide apart, in the coffin underneath the hole while Lubchik landed, in similarly ungainly fashion, inside a second open coffin across the vaulted chamber. Both of the wooden stakes contained within the skeletons were sent flying.

At the same time, hell-bent on freedom, wolf after wolf leaped headlong through the secret entrance. All of them uncaring which direction they took, fell sprawling in coffins all around the chamber.

"No, no, my darlings!" cried Count Alucard in desperation. "Not inside the caskets of my ancestors!"

But the younger wolves paid him not the slightest attention, while the elders, who would have liked to have been mindful of his words, were unable to prevent themselves. Soon, there was not a coffin in the vaulted chamber that did not contain at least one wolf – and, more to the point, there was not a pointed stake that was not dislodged . . .

"Oh, no!" wailed Count Alucard, aghast at what was happening. "Oh, *no* . . .!"

Then, as the candles flickered eerily in their sconces, there came a sudden whirring sound accompanied by a long, low concerted groan which caused the wolves to leap to the floor. Out of every coffin, on widespread, ominous, black membraneous wing, there rose a vampire bat. While the floor of the vaulted chamber was a seething mass of snarling, snapping, jostling wolves, the air above was thick with hovering blood-seeking Alucards of old, returned to life.

It was, of course, the quick-witted Boris who, though wide-eyed with fear, managed to stumble up the worn flight of steps, beyond which lay both the forest and the theme park.

"Ah-whoo-**OOOH**-oooooh . . .!"

One by one, following the pack-leader's example, the wolves scrambled, stumbled and then fell over each other's paws in their anxiety, as they headed up the worn stone steps towards the open door and the sweet-scented smell of evening air. The bats, also sniffing freedom in their nostrils, zoomed and zapped above the heads of the wolves.

Seconds later, with the candle flames now burning steadily, the tomb stood silent and empty – except for the crumpled figure of Count Alucard, whose slim shoulders drooped, having watched both wolves and vampires take off into the night.

"Oh, heavens," the Count murmured glumly, gazing at the rows of empty coffins. "Now there really *will* be trouble."

Under ordinary circumstances, having struck open air at last, the wolves' natural instincts would have led them into the forest which lay just beyond the ancient vaults. The circumstances though were anything but ordinary. The entire pack was in a panic. There were any number of vampire bats darting directly overhead. The wolves had been cooped up in total blackness inside the secret passage for far too long . . .

It was understandable then, that for all of these reasons, instead of turning right and heading for the fringe of friendly bushes that marked the edge of the forest, the entire pack veered left and bounded towards Vampire Park – at the very moment that Lord Freddie gave the signal for the theme park's illuminations to be switched on.

The vampire bats were also in a state of some confusion. They had been awakened, unceremoniously, from a sleep which, for some of them, had lasted several centuries. They had returned to living consciousness to find their resting place invaded by a pack of seemingly half-crazed wolves. It was also understandable then that, instead of heading for the friendly dark and wide expanses of Tolokovin Forest, the vampires took their lead from the wolf-pack and zoomed, on outstretched wing, on course for Vampire Park.

"Hurrah!"

Unaware of the fast-approaching double danger of wolves and vampires, the Tolokovinite peasants clustered in the theme park's main square let out a concerted roar of approval as the several thousand coloured lights twinkled into life. The floodlit "VAMPIRE CASTLE" sign was also blazing brightly.

At that same moment, taking the "switch-on" as his cue, Butch Brannigan, again harnessed to the high steel wire, launched himself on outstretched plastic wings for his second public performance.

It was unfortunate for the make-believe Count Alucard that, halfway down the wire, he suddenly found himself surrounded by some half-dozen or so *real* vampire bats. The vampires flapped and fluttered around the stuntman's head, their razor-sharp, pearl-white fangs glistening in the theme park's lights.

"Go away! Get off!" cried Brannigan, fluttering and flapping his own ungainly wings in a vain attempt to dispel his assailants. "Go bother somebody else!" he wailed. But in his anxiety to rid himself of the vampire bats' attentions, he succeeded only in coming to a complete stop himself. As the stuntman hung suspended by his harness high above the theme park, the vampires, seeking only to escape themselves but blinded by the bright lights, continued to harass and torment him as they wheeled and squealed and pivoted around his head.

"Hurrah!"

The crowd below, their faces upturned, believing that what they were watching was all part and parcel of the evening's entertainment, continued to applaud and cheer the unfortunate Butch Brannigan. Their enjoyment was short-lived however when the wolf-pack bounded onto the scene.

"Ah-whoo-OOOH-oooooh . . .!"

The wolves, following close behind the vampire bats and still panicky, were even more distraught at finding themselves in the floodlit theme park. Like the dark-winged vampires that wheeled and shrieked in the sky above, the wolves were eager to return to the privacy of the wide-ranging forest. Having escaped from the steel-mesh fenced enclosure, they now found themselves contained within another prison – the brightly-lit palisade-ringed Vampire Park. Not only that, but they were surrounded on all sides by those creatures they despised above all other living things – human beings.

Their desperation increasing by the second, the wolves charged hither and thither through the theme park, scattering groups of terrified Tolokovinite peasants who were as fearful of the wolf-pack as the wolf-pack was of them.

And, while wolves and peasants ran in all directions, suspended on his harness and marooned above the theme park, Butch Brannigan continued to thresh his plastic wings in terror, as wave after wave of temporarily blinded vampire bats blundered into his face and body.

"Help me! *Please*! Somebody help me!" wailed the stuntman.

But Butch Brannigan's desperate cries for assistance went unanswered. For there was no one there to help him. Certainly not Lord Freddie, nor the butler, Higgins, for they had problems of their own to deal with . . .

At the same moment that he had given the signal for the switching-on of the theme park's lights, Lord Freddie had taken up his position in the front seat of the leading coach for the very first trip on the park's main attraction: the vampire roller-coaster.

The only passengers allowed on board The Vampire Ride on this inaugral journey were those persons that Lord Freddie deemed sufficiently important to accompany him. Sitting beside his lordship was his butler, Higgins, and behind these two sat Mayor Henri Rumboll, in all of his regalia, and Police Sergeant Alphonse Kropotel, his medals gleaming. Both of the rear seats in the leading coach were taken up by the portly grocer, Eric Horowitz. All the coaches that followed were empty which, in view of the events that were speedily to follow, was a good thing for all of those peasants who wished themselves on board.

The vampire rollercoaster had been much publicised as a "thrill-a-second ride" – but the five passengers occupying the front coach in that very first journey would remember it for the rest of their days as the most terrifying experience of their lives. For years to come they would start up in their beds at night, pyjamas soaked with sweat, having relived that awful ride in their worst nightmares.

At a second imperious hand signal from Lord Freddie, the peasant in charge of the rollercoaster (whose name was Jacob Kroll,) tugged at the controlling lever and the line of coaches started out. Slowly at first, as is the way with all rollercoasters and seeming to struggle as it mounted the first steep upward incline then, with all five passengers gripping tight onto their handrails, the leading coach breasted the ride's first summit and rattled breathtakingly down the other side.

It was at this point that the vampire rollercoaster's inaugral ride took on a fiendishly nightmare quality that its inventor had not devised. As the first coach levelled and juddered along for several metres just above the ground, a couple of wolves appeared as if from nowhere and leaped up, snarling and howling at the horrified passengers.

"Yee-aaah-AAAGH . . .!" yelled the VIPs in

unison, their knuckles showing white as they tightened their grips on the handrails, their hearts pounding.

Then, no sooner had they left the snapping, slobbering wolves behind but, as they clattered swiftly up the next sharp incline, they found themselves eyeball-to-bulging-eyeball with several hovering vampire bats.

"Yee-aaah-OOOOH . . .!" screamed the five unfortunates as the real-life vampire bats fluttered in their faces.

The same awful pattern continued, without pause, as the coaches careered and rattled around the track. At every low point there were waiting wolves positioned to leap and snap at the terrified passengers while, at every incline's summit, there were hovering dazzled bats to slap into their faces.

Worst of all though, the gruesome ride was not to end after a single circuit as its maker had intended. Jacob Kroll, having spotted the wolves and vampires through the window of his cabin, had ducked beneath the control counter for his own protection. Without Kroll's guiding hand on the brake lever, the rollercoaster continued travelling round and round, up and down, the passengers harassed by wolves and dive-bombed by vampire bats time after time and circuit after circuit . . .

In the farthest, shadowy corner of the vaulted underground burial chamber, Count Alucard held the flickering candle close to the coffin lid as he peered closely at the words which were inscribed on

173

it. Just to be on the safe side, he read them through for a second time.

"Henry was right!" the Count murmured to himself. " 'Lord' Freddie is not a lord at all. Neither is he my cousin. He is both rogue and fraud."

Then, rising to his full height, the Count replaced the candle in its ancient sconce and walked purposefully up the stone steps, out into the warm night air.

Count Alucard was not at all surprised to find Vampire Park deserted and strangely silent under its blazing floodlights. It did not take him long to guess, rightly, what had happened.

While the other wolves had dashed aimlessly around the theme park, throwing the peasants into confusion, harassing the passengers on the rollercoaster and, in doing both of these things, had succeeded only in becoming more harassed and confused themselves – their leader, Boris, had managed to get his own fears of the brightly-lit and crowded Vampire Park under some sort of control. Not only that, but in snuffling his way round the palisade, he had found a spot where two of the palings were missing. Peering through the gap in the tall wooden fence, Boris had been relieved to glimpse the dark and welcoming safety of his homeland, the forest.

"Ah-whoo-OOOOH . . .!"

Hearing their pack-leader's urgent howl, the wolves, one by one and young and old, had paused at whatever mischief they were up to, turned in the direction from which the sound had come, ears pricked, tongues lolling.

"Ah-whoo-OOOOOOH . . .!"

This time, having gained the pack's attention, Boris slipped through the gap that he had found. In ones and twos, twos and threes, and even threes and fours, the Tolokovin wolves loped after their leader, scrabbling through the hole to be quickly lost from sight in the trees beyond.

The Tolokovin peasants – both theme park staff and visitors alike – stunned by the wolf-pack's sudden exit, had stood stock-still for several seconds before heading, en masse, towards the park's main gates. Leaving their parked transport behind, but carrying the carters along with them, they had fled, as fast as their legs would carry them, away from the horrors of the theme park and along the moonlit road that meandered down to Tolokovin.

The vampires meanwhile, still blinded by the theme park's floodlights and fluttering aimlessly, had picked up the sound of the peasants' exodus with their keen bats' hearing and, regrouping, had flapped off in close formation in the same direction.

The sound of beating bats' wings overhead had spurred the fleeing peasants into even faster head-long flight.

Sensing that danger had passed, Jacob Kroll lifted his head and peered nervously over the top of the rollercoaster's control panel. He looked out through the observation window. He was right, he congratulated himself. Both vampires and wolves were gone. But the rollercoaster, with its five fearful, white-faced Very Important Passengers all clinging grimly to their respective handrails in the leading coach, was still rattling round, and round, and round, and round . . .

Joseph Kroll got to his feet, applied the brake and, slowly, the rollercoaster clattered to a halt.

Seconds later, "Lord" Freddie Allardyce Alucard, Higgins the butler, Mayor Henri Rumboll, Police Sergeant Alphonse Kropotel and Eric Horowitz, the portly Tolokovin grocer, were stumbling towards the theme park's main gates. They were joined, en route, by the plastic-winged Butch Brannigan who, in a similar state of nervous near-collapse, had managed to edge his way down the taut steel wire.

Not a word passed between them as they scampered out through the gates of Vampire Park and then down the mountain road in the wake of the fast-disappearing peasants.

"Count Alucard!" cried Henry Hollins joyfully as he opened the door of the theme park's gift shop. "I was beginning to wonder what had happened to you."

"I am extraordinarily well and in most excellent spirits, all thanks to you, my dear young friend," replied the Count. "Your suspicions were well founded. I have been down into the family tomb and studied the inscription on the coffin lid of my much-travelled evil ancestor. It contains a brief but nonetheless comprehensive account of his life. You were quite correct, Henry. There was no English bride. He never married. Consequently, there is no English branch of the Alucard family. 'Lord'

177

Freddie, as he chooses to call himself, is a fraud. So is the will – it is worth no more than the fake parchment it is written on."

"And so you are the real owner of Alucard Castle?"

"I always was," said Count Alucard, smiling happily. "But let us speak no more of my concerns – what of your problems? I have wandered all across Vampire Park and it is quite deserted. I am fearful, my young friend, for the safety of your dear parents."

"Oh, *they're* all right," said Henry Hollins, opening the gift shop door a little wider. "And so are the other foreign tourists. They're all in here. I went out and found them when I first heard the shouts of 'Vampires!'."

"Well done!" exclaimed the Count.

"Mum! Dad! Everyone!" called Henry Hollins. "It's quite safe now. Come out and meet Count Alucard."

A moment later, Albert and Emily Hollins came out of the darkness of the gift shop, blinking at the theme park's bright lights. Following them, a shade nervously, came Hans and Frieda Grunwald with their little daughter, Greta; Franco and Rosa Granelli and, lastly, holding hands, the shy Welsh honeymooners, Ivor and Bronwyn Williams.

"Welcome to Castle Alucard!" announced the Count, trying hard not to laugh.

Every one of the tourists was wearing white face-paint and had painted red-rimmed eyes. They also had vampire plastic teeth jutting over their lower lips and vampire plastic blood-stained fingernails dangling from their hands.

"I thought it might be a good idea to disguise them all as vampires," explained Henry Hollins. "And then, if they were to come across any *real* vampires, they might not get bitten."

"Congratulations to you on an excellent scheme, my young friend," declared Count Alucard. "Although, to let you into a little secret, there is nothing to be feared from my fluttering ancestors. They have slept too long in their coffins to present any immediate danger. Their appearance is much worse than their bite. It would require several days for them to gain sufficient strength to bite anyone."

"But what will happen to the villagers when that time comes?" asked Henry, showing some concern.

"It won't," the Count replied firmly. "When dawn breaks they will return to their coffins and assume again their skeleton forms. I shall see to it that the stakes are replaced in their bones."

"All's well that ends well," said Emily Hollins comfortably.

"But it is not yet ended, my dear lady," said the Count, extending his long thin arms to take in the brightly-lit theme park. "Tomorrow I shall start to make enquiries about having all of this taken down – but tonight, and while you are all my guests, we must not allow it to be wasted. Which of the theme park's many pleasures would you all care to try out first?"

"Can you work the Vampire Park ride, Count?" asked Henry Hollins, with a little excited gulp.

"I believe I do possess that ability," said Count Alucard gravely. "Follow me."

Then, with his scarlet-lined black cloak billowing out behind him, Count Alucard led his foreign

179

visitors across the floodlit theme park and towards the waiting coaches of the Transylvanian rollercoaster.

"Help! Help, *please* – Help!"

Count Alucard paused and cocked a listening ear. He thought that he recognized the voice that called out for assistance – he was not yet sure from which direction the cry had come?

It was not long after dawn. The sun's first rays were filtering through the trees. The scent of pine needles hung on the still, crisp air. The Count was taking his usual early morning stroll in the forest.

"Help! Someone – *anyone*!" It was a different voice that cried out this time, but from the same direction as the first. "*Help* – will somebody kindly come to our assistance?" This third call came from yet another throat and Count Alucard was now convinced he knew the owners of all three voices.

"*Ah–whoo. OOOOOOH . . . .!*"

The wolf-howl echoed in the trees and, having a good idea of what he might expect to find, Count Alucard strode out on his spindly legs in the direction that he judged the men's cries and the animal's howl to have come from. It did not take him long to discover that exact location.

"Good morning, Freddie!" cried the Count, peering up at the man who had pretended to be his cousin and who was now perched, uncomfortably, some several metres up a pine tree. "Good morning, Mr Higgins! Good morning, Mr Brannigan!" he added, smiling up at those last-named two gentlemen who were also occupying branches in the tree. "I thought you three had left Tolokovin last evening," the Count continued. "What on earth are you doing sitting up there?"

"You can *see* why we're here, you Transylvanian monster!" wailed Freddie, his arms wrapped tightly around the tree-trunk. "We're cold, we're hungry and we've been stuck up here all night – all because of your bloodthirsty beasts!"

Count Alucard bit back a smile and looked down at his friends, the wolves, who were sitting on their haunches in a circle round the tree. Staring gravely up at their captives, the wolves stretched wide their jaws occasionally, showing their glistening fangs and allowing the odd globule of saliva to spill onto the ground.

The Count guessed at what had happened – in their flight from the castle on the previous afternoon, Freddie and his two accomplices must have split up from Mayor Rumboll and Sergeant Kropotel, lost themselves in the forest and then come across the wolf-pack . . .

"Can't you call them off, Count Alucard?" whimpered Higgins. "My arms are aching and I've got pins-and-needles in my legs."

"Something is crawling round the back of my neck," sniffed Brannigan. "I think it's some sort of spider." The stuntman looked a sorry sight. In his haste to flee the castle he had not had time to take off his plastic wings and, torn and broken, they hung down his back.

"I beg of you, Count Alucard," sobbed Freddie, hugging hard on the tree. "Call those frightful animals off and, I give you my solemn word you will never set eyes on us again."

Count Alucard did not reply immediately. For several seconds he wondered whether or not to leave the three men where they were for just a little longer? But he dismissed the thought as quickly as it had come. They had, he told himself, suffered enough already. The Count was not an unkind man, neither was he the sort of chap that needs to get his own back on anyone who has done him an injustice.

"You can come down from there whenever you feel like it," the Count assured the trembling threesome. "The wolves won't hurt you – not unless you attempt to harm them first. They have never wilfully so much as nipped a human person in their entire existence. Although, believe me, they have had good reason to do so on more than one occasion."

Strangely enough, although Freddie, Higgins and Butch Brannigan knew full well that Count Alucard did not owe them any favours, they also knew him well enough to know that he would not lie to them. Count Alucard was a truthful person. Shamefacedly, the three men scrambled to the ground and straightway set off – without so much as a glance at the Count – walking quickly at first, then breaking into a run, soon to be lost from sight in the forest.

"Come on, old friend," murmured Count Alucard, lowering a hand and scratching at the loose greying fur under Boris's jowls. "There is just sufficient time for me to complete my stroll before I must return to the castle for breakfast with those dear, good folk, the Hollinses."

A moment later, Count Alucard was almost out

of sight, striding off in the opposite direction to the one taken by the three men and with a score and more of wolves leaping and bounding at his heels.

One good thing that had to be said about "Cousin" Freddie and his two henchmen was that they kept to their word and were never ever seen again in Transylvania.

EPILOGUE

As the first rays of the early morning sun crept into his cell through the high arched window, Count Alucard woke in his cosy coffin to the sound of urgent hammering outside.

"Good!" he exclaimed, then added: "Indeed – excellent!"

Some weeks had passed since his visitors had left and now the workmen had arrived from the city to begin dismantling the theme park's many structures.

It had been agreed between the Count and the firm engaged to do the work that they would be entitled to keep all of the rides and buildings they were taking down, to be erected again in some more suitable environment, provided that they returned the castle's precincts to the pleasing rural state they had presented prior to "Lord" Freddie's arrival. And the very first thing that was to be demolished, Count Alucard had insisted, was the fence that had contained the "wolf enclosure".

"Ah-whoo-OOOOH . . .!"

The distant howl from a wandering lone wolf reminded the Count that it was time for him to get out of his coffin. After a breakfast of fresh peaches and plums washed down with a glass of tomato juice spiced with Worcester sauce, he told himself, he might very well take himself off into the forest to see how the pack was enjoying its freedom. And then, in the afternoon, he might sit down and drop a line to Henry Hollins, inviting his young friend and his charming parents back to Alucard Castle for a proper holiday . . .

"If anyone wants me urgently, Glenda," said Donald Macintosh as he hoisted his bag of golf clubs onto his shoulder, "you can get me on my mobile phone at the golf club . . ."

But as the travel agent moved towards the agency door it was opened from outside and Emily Hollins entered, wearing a big smile, a comfortable skirt, white socks, sneakers and a T-shirt emblazoned with the legend:

I'VE BEEN TO
VAMPIRE PARK
AND ALL
THAT I CAME BACK WITH
WERE
THIS LOUSY T-SHIRT AND
TWO BITE-MARKS ON MY NECK!

"Good morning, Mrs Hollins," said Mr Macintosh in slightly hollow tones. "I imagine you've called in to tell me all about your Transylvanian trip?"

"Mmmm – partly that," said Emily, heading towards a chair. "And partly to talk about our next

185

year's holiday. I thought we might start organizing things in good time for once."

"Jolly good," said Mr Macintosh glumly as he lowered his bag of golf clubs to the floor.

Elsa Hoggel, a goose's carcase draped over the lap of her black apron, was sitting on a three-legged stool outside her own front door. She glanced up and down the empty cobbled street and then grunted with approval. She was glad to see Tolokovin empty of tourists. Foreign visitors were all very well as a means of earning oneself the odd extra grobek but, all things considered, the old woman preferred to keep herself to herself.

"I'm getting too old to sleep in the hen house," she grumbled to herself.

Besides, foreigners were difficult to understand. Why, for instance, had her last visitors, the Hollinses, taken down the picture of Saint Unfortunato from above the big brass double bed and hidden it in the wardrobe? Frau Hoggel, mystified, shook her head.

Then, dismissing the incident from her mind, she set to work with a will, plucking the goose's carcase.

Within seconds, Elsa Hoggel was hidden in a cloud of goose feathers.

Karl Gustaffe, Tolokovin's master-baker, untied the red spotted handkerchief from around his neck and used it to mop his brow.

Some men hanker after the great outdoors and seek to feel the wind in their hair – Karl Gustaffe was only truly happy in the sweltering heat of his tiny bakehouse. He glanced around with great satisfaction. Although the morning was only half-way gone, he had already baked one hundred and twenty-five shrubel-cakes; there were another one hundred and twenty-five browning in the oven; and there was sufficient dough in his mixing-bowl to make yet another one hundred and twenty-five.

The next day was a feast day in Tolokovin. The feast day of Saint Unfortunato himself! Everyone ate shrubel-cake on Saint Unfortunato's Day. It would be possible for Karl Gustaffe to sell as many shrubel-cakes as he was able to bake.

Pleased with life, the baker began to sing, softly, the words of an old Transylvanian folk-song:

> "Sovra zora,
> Sovora dovra-dovrey,
> Sovra zokra,
> Sovola zokrato . . ."

Emil Gruff was scowling as he strode through the forest, his axe slung over his shoulder, its blade glinting in the sunlight which was filtering through the trees.

The woodcutter had not smiled now for several weeks. This was good, he told himself. Gruff's red-bearded weather-beaten features were not best suited to a smile, whereas a frown sat easily on his face. He was on his way to perform his second favourite task. He was going to chop down a pine tree. He would have dearly loved to have chopped down the entire Forest of Tolokovin – but the forest was so wide-ranging that the trees grew faster than Emil Gruff could bring them to the ground.

The woodcutter's most favourite task was trapping wolves. But that also had its problems. As fast as he set his traps, some oaf went out at night and sprang them. Emil Gruff had a good idea as to that rogue's identity. Alas, he could not prove it . . .

"Excuse me, Emil Gruff!"

The woodcutter, lost in angry thought, had not noticed Count Alucard striding lightly towards him on the forest path. As the Count stepped briskly past Gruff, and then on his way along the woodland path, the woodcutter's scowl deepened as he glanced over his shoulder.

"Vile satanic blood-sucker!" shouted Emil Gruff after the fast-disappearing Count. "Accursed devil of darkness!"

Count Alucard heard but did not mind the woodcutter's name-calling. You knew exactly where you were when Emil Gruff scowled and shouted insults. It was when Gruff smiled and passed the time of day with you that you needed to be on your guard.

Count Alucard smiled, dismissing the woodcutter from his thoughts. The Count was going to see his friends, the wolves. Although there was no sign of them, he sensed that they were gathered in the clearing just around the next bend in the forest path.

"Ah-whoo-OOOOOOH . . .!"

Count Alucard's smile broadened. He quickened his pace. His spirits rose. Then, as he turned into the clearing and every single member of the Tolokovin Forest wolf-pack sprang towards him, Count Alucard threw open his arms in welcome.